Friendship Meadow

*Where Friendship Is
an Everyday Thing*

Christian Homestead Press
8655 CR 318
Shreve, Ohio, 44676

ISBN:0-9787031-1-1

Author: Rex B. Dye
Illustrated by: Anne Brush

Written 1973
Revised 2008

Carlisle Printing

Table Of Contents

Dedication

Friendship Meadow was written long years ago for a little nine-year-old girl named Melanie, who loved her father through difficult times. Today she is a mature young woman with her own family. The years have not diminished her loving nature. Today she has developed into a very strong servant of the Lord with her own love, compassion, and friendship for children.

Now, many years later, this book and its story are dedicated to her, with the hope that all who read it will gain a deeper sense of the need for loving friendship in this world.

Recognition & Thanks

It is with great appreciation and thankfulness that we recognize the excellent artistic work of Anne Brush. Her illustrations of various characters in this book capture not only the essence of their nature, but the setting and tension of some of the most important scenes described in our story.

Anne's ability to envision the personalities and their actions in the course of this tale is unique, and her ability to transfer those visions into visible representations is outstanding. Again, thank you, Anne!

CHAPTER 1

Wake Up! Digby

HIS BEDROOM WAS very, very dark. His bed was very, very warm, and it was oh, so snug. Digby was terribly comfortable. He had really no reason to wake up. But through his sweet slumber, Digby thought he could hear a tiny voice that kept saying, "Get up, Digby! Digby –

it's time to get up."

Digby had been asleep for quite a long while. It was really past time when he should have been up and about. Again came the tiny voice; "Wake up! You sleepyhead, wake up!" It seemed for some reason that the voice was getting louder. Digby rolled over and covered his ears. He thought to himself, "Now that will take care of you, whoever you are."

It was not in Digby's nature to be in much of a hurry doing anything. Getting awake after a long, peaceful snooze was one thing at which he was especially slow in doing. In fact, if that pesky voice would leave him alone, Digby thought, he would just go on sleeping and sleeping.

"Digby! Digby! Open your eyes!" There it was again. But how could that be? Hadn't he covered his ears tightly with his paws?

"Paws!" you say. Why certainly paws, for you see, Digby's full name was Digby C. Groundhog. The "C." stood for "Charles," after his grandfather. Some at times called him "Chuck" as a nickname. Yes, Digby was a furry little groundhog.

You should know, if you don't, that in the north country it is the habit of groundhogs to sleep through most of the long, icy winter months. As the weather turns cold and the snow comes on the howling northwest winds, the groundhog, like many other animals, begins to get a strange feeling deep inside which tells him that it is time to crawl way down into his underground home, curl up in his snug little bedroom, and drop off into his winter nap.

Now, once more, Digby was being stirred by that

voice from somewhere deep inside. It was getting louder and louder. "Wake up, you lazy groundhog," it said. "You have slept long enough – Get UP!" For a moment nothing happened. Then the very tip of Digby's nose wiggled. Once more. Then twice. An eyelid fluttered. Just one, that was for sure, but it fluttered. Now the voice came like a drumbeat: "Up! Up! – Get up, Digby! DIGBY CHARLES GROUNDHOG! GET OUT OF BED!"

Digby had never gone to school and had not been taught much about animals, so he did not know much about that voice that was rousing him from his sleep. He did not know that the voice was not some nasty person playing a joke on him. He did not know that the voice was his own instinct, his own natural clock telling him that it was time to wake up.

Just in case you have not learned yet what an "instinct" is, let us just say that it is a strong feeling placed in animals by the Mighty God who created all things – a feeling that helps guide their lives. As you get older you will learn much more about instinct in animals.

As for Digby, his instinct had done its job well. It had wakened him from his long winter's nap. Both of his eyes were open now – droopy, yes, but open.

A bit later Digby struggled up to a sitting position. Slowly at first he placed a foot on the floor, and then one by one, the other three. Very shakily he stood on legs that had not been used for some time. After getting his balance, Digby began to tidy up his room and make his bed. That was the way he had been taught. He always felt better when he could look around and see a neat and tidy room.

Then, in no hurry, Digby made his way slowly up the long hallway to his front door. During the winter it had been covered over first by leaves and then by snow. The snow was gone now, but he had to push his way through the leaves out into the open. The sunshine was oh, so bright. The little groundhog could hardly keep his eyes open. Only by squinting could he see anything for a while. Then his eyes got used to the light and he began to look around warily. This was his habit.

Every time Digby came out of his house he went through the same actions. First he looked all around and then sniffed the air. He had to do those things to be safe, because in his world, just like ours, there are bad characters who do not treat other folks nicely. Sad as it is, even a harmless little animal like Digby has enemies.

There are other creatures in the meadow where he lived who would enjoy catching him unaware and doing him harm. One of his worst enemies was an odd-looking creature who used only two of his four legs for walking. He carried what some of the meadow folk called a "magic stick," which made a terribly loud noise and frightened the folks of the woodland badly. Once in a while when it sounded, one of the folks would suddenly fall down and never move again.

After looking about and seeing no danger, the furry little fellow crawled all the way out onto his front porch and began enjoying the warm sunshine. He loved to look at the blue sky and the little fluffy white clouds floating up there. "Whoever made those really knew how to make beautiful things!" Digby thought to himself. After a few minutes, he spoke out loud, "Now I am glad that little voice woke me up. It is a beautiful day!"

Digby had been taking his ease there in front of his house for about half an hour. But even while he relaxed, his senses were always tuned to any unusual sound or movement that might signal danger. As he gazed up into the sky, the shape of a small cloud reminded him of a large clump of sweet clover shoots. The longer he thought about it, the hungrier he got.

Just as Digby came to a decision to go looking for some food, a rustling in the weeds a few yards away sent him tumbling and falling all over himself to get into the front door of his house.

The terrified groundhog landed on his head a few feet down his front hallway, with stones and dirt pouring down on him. To make things worse, he had forgotten to close his mouth. As he picked himself up off the floor he sputtered and coughed, trying to get the sand out of his teeth. At the same time he rubbed a very tender spot on the top of his head where he had just made a perfect one-point landing.

After collecting himself and smoothing out some bumps and bruises, the woodchuck, (that is what groundhogs are sometimes called) began to fall under one of his family's most dangerous weaknesses – curiosity. Slowly but surely he began to creep back up to the doorway of his house. Having reached the door, he waited a moment and then quickly popped his head out and looked around.

If the noise had been made by that odd creature that walks around on two legs, Digby would have been in great danger. Digby had heard some of the other woodsfolk call that creature, "man". It was an odd name, he thought. But what the groundhog didn't know was that the man knows the groundhog family's habits, and uses this knowledge so he can use that magic stick against them — the thing that made the terrible noise.

Digby wondered why he had heard a zipping - whistling noise close above his head a couple of times when that stick made the big noise. He thought there must have been some connection between the two. By now, though, he knew that the thing was dangerous and that he had to be very watchful of it.

Digby looked all about but could see nothing that looked dangerous. He said to himself, "I wonder what that could have been. I'm certain I heard a strange noise. Oh! Maybe I am not really awake yet — maybe I'm still dreaming."

At that moment a high-pitched giggle came rolling out of the weeds above Digby's front door. "He-e-e-he-he-ha! What's the matter, you old sleepyhead? You're kind of jittery, aren't you?" Digby looked up just in time to see, laughing down at him, a gray, furry face with a pointed nose, big round eyes, and two long, loppy, crooked, hanging ears.

"Bouncer!" Digby squealed. "Good old Bouncer! Oh! It's so good to see you!"

"It's good to see you too, Digby, my friend. We thought for a while you were going to sleep all summer."

The little groundhog's face was smiles all over, and his shiny black nose just couldn't stop wiggling with happiness at seeing his good friend, Bouncer Rabbit. But suddenly a very serious expression came over Digby's face. "Bouncer, please don't ever scare me like that again! I fell right down my hallway and got a mouthful of sand, not to mention a big bump on my head. That was a dirty trick you played on me, you mischievous rabbit."

At that Bouncer laughed and rolled in the early spring grass until big rabbit tears rolled down his furry cheeks. A fit of squeaky rabbit coughs laid him flat on his back. "Oh-ho-ha-ha, I know, Digby, but I just couldn't pass up the chance when I saw you sitting there so content with the world. I am sorry – really I am."

"Well, all right, Bouncer, I forgive you. Forgiving is a good thing to do. But the next time, come in by my front yard where I can see you."

"Thank you, Digby, I certainly will. By the way, my friend, you look terribly thin. Have you had anything to eat?"

"Oh! My goodness, Bouncer! I was just about to go and find something for lunch, but you came along and frightened me and I forgot all about it. Yes! I am hungry! Very hungry! Hey! Will you come along to dinner with me?"

"Why, I don't mind if I do, my furry friend. Now where shall we dine? Up at the Hilltop Lounge? Or down at the Green Valley Inn?"

"Well, I believe, Bouncer, it would be best if we went down to the Green Valley Inn, because my legs are so weak right now that I don't think I could make it to the top of the hill. Shall we go?"

"It is a beautiful day," Digby thought. "The sun is

shining, the blue sky is powdery with fluffy white clouds, and a good friend is at my side. It's good to be alive and awake!"

CHAPTER 2

Big Mouth and the Professor

IN THE EARLY springtime, small blades of grass and sprigs of clover and alfalfa peek through the dead weeds of the past summer. These young plants are very tender and juicy. So tender and juicy are they that many of the woodsfolk can hardly wait for springtime so they can feast upon them. Now that the magical time of the year had come, the sound of munching and chomping could be heard coming from almost every clump of greenery in sight.

Digby and Bouncer did not waste much time getting to the valley meadow and their tasty meal. As they munched away they talked from time to time about fluffy clouds, and about many of their neighbors.

"Digby, did you know that Chatty Squirrel, Skippy Chipmunk, and Ringo Coon each had narrow escapes from that strange thing that walks on two legs?" Bouncer asked.

"Why, no, Bouncer, what happened?" Digby inquired in between mouthfuls of tender greens.

"Well, my friend, it seems that Two Legs, which is what everybody calls him now, has certain seasons of the year when he intentionally tries to kill some of us. For others of us, he just tries to do that any time he feels like it," Bouncer replied.

"My goodness!" interrupted Digby, "I thought the only seasons were seasons of the year like summer - fall - winter and spring. I never knew there were seasons for killing! Oh! My goodness!"

"Yes, Digby, it sounds ridiculous, but what is still more disturbing is that even some animals take pleasure in harming other animals, even killing them. Anyway, it seems that last fall, about the time you were getting ready to go to bed for the winter, it came the season when Two Legs hunts for squirrels. Chatty Squirrel had gotten up at her usual time and had left her home for a short journey to the hickory tree. You know she just loves hickory nuts."

Bouncer stuffed another large bunch of alfalfa sprouts

into his cheek and continued. "As Chatty was making her way through the branches of a large oak tree, she thought she noticed a flash of color on the ground below which did not belong in the forest scenery." The rabbit stopped for a moment and chewed for a short time, and then continued. "She jumped behind a large limb, and just in time too, for a second later a terrible roaring sound tore through the woods. And with it came a hundred little zipping, pecking sounds showering all around where Chatty was hiding."

"Wow!" Digby whistled, his eyes all round and bugging out. "What was it, Bouncer? Was Chatty hurt? Was she afraid?"

Bouncer held up both front paws and said, "Whoa— Whoa! Wait a minute. One question at a time." Bouncer finished swallowing and continued.

"No, Chatty wasn't hurt because she was well hidden. Yes, she was frightened, as any of us would be. And I don't know what it was exactly that made the pecking sounds, but many of us believe it was something that comes from that stick that makes the big noise."

Digby sat thinking for a moment, took another mouthful of clover and chewed, and thought for a longer time. After a while he said, "I agree. That stick, the big noise, and those mysterious zipping, whistling, pecking sounds are somehow connected. But, back to Chatty. How did she escape?"

Bouncer leaned back in the warm sunshine, rested against a big rock, and continued. "Welll-l-l-l", he drawled, "It seems that Two Legs isn't too bright. As soon as Chatty popped out of sight on the side of the tree away from Two

Legs, he began to circle around the tree trying to catch sight of Chatty, but she outsmarted him.

As he moved around the tree, so did she, always keeping the tree between herself and Two Legs. They went round and round the tree so many times that Two Legs started to get dizzy. Finally, he was certain that Chatty had somehow gotten off the tree without him seeing her. So after traveling around the tree a couple more times, the disgusted hunter sneaked off through the woods looking for someone else to attack."

"Oh! Good!" Digby squealed, clapping his paws. "I'm so glad Chatty fooled Two Legs. That is what he deserves!"

Now Digby found himself a comfortable seat, rubbed his tightly stretched tummy, sighed, and muttered, "It's such a fine day. By the way, Bouncer, you mentioned that both Skippy and Ringo had close calls too with Two Legs. What was that all about?"

"Yes, well, you see, their experiences were similar," Bouncer began. "Ringo went out for a late night stroll and got chased by Two Legs' dog. He made it to a hollow tree just in the nick of time. As for Skippy, he was just out playing in the leaves when suddenly the ground seemed to explode right in front of his nose. At the same instant, a frightful sound tore through the woods. It was Two Legs' noisy stick of course. Skippy wasn't bothering anyone. I just don't understand Two Legs at all!"

The two friends grew silent for a time and both were growing very drowsy in the warm springtime sun. Suddenly a screeching, squalling commotion erupted from the trees and brush not far from where Digby and Bouncer were resting. For an instant both of them froze in their reclining positions, but the next moment they sprang instinctively into a nearby clump of prickly briars and timothy grass.

The two frightened friends crouched out of sight, listening and looking, and sniffing the air. Both were trying to locate and identify the source of the uproar. Until they knew for certain what it was, they had to be very, very careful. It might be a great danger for them.

They listened for a short time to the squawking and squalling, then they glanced at each other with a glint of laughter in their eyes. "They're at it again," Digby sighed, "they're at it again. They can't wait until a person is fully awake before they start after each other."

"Sure enough," the rabbit agreed, "it's them, but it is really Big Mouth Bertie making all the noise. The Professor never fusses back, you know."

"Yes, that's right, but he has a way of driving Bertie into a frenzy. It's partly his fault too," Digby replied.

"Hey, come on," Bouncer cried, "let's go down and watch. What do you say?"

"OK," the groundhog grunted as he got up. "The show those two put on is usually a lot of fun to watch."

The groundhog and the rabbit made their way to the line of trees and beyond into the cool, dark woods. The sounds of the conflict grew louder as they drew closer.

"They must be at that big old pine tree that stands beside the mossy rock," panted Digby. He had grown badly out of condition during his long winter nap. He wheezed, "Slow down, Bouncer!"

"What's the matter, Digby, are you getting tired? It's

just a short way yet," came the reply.

The two arrived at the scene of the battle just in time to see Big Mouth Bertie Crow make two or three sweeping passes at the top of the big pine tree. As he dived and swooped he kept up a continuous screeching, "Caw-w-w-w-w, Caw-w, Caw-caw-caw!" He would fly at the top of the tree, screeching as he came. At the very last moment, just as it seemed he would crash into the dense branches, Bertie would veer up and away, only to circle and start another dive.

For a short time Digby and Bouncer could not make out the object of the crow's anger. Then, as they looked closer, they could just see a dark figure huddled high up in the pine tree, sheltered by its heavy foliage.

"There's the Professor all right!" Bouncer exclaimed.

"Yes, I see him," said Digby. "I wonder how long he will sit there and listen to that racket?"

Bouncer thought for a moment, then said, "Quite a while I suppose. I've heard tell that the Professor can't see very well in the daylight, so I suppose he will wait until dark to make a move."

At that moment a tiny voice from the top of a nearby hazelnut bush piped up. "Don't you believe that, Digby, Professor Wiseman Owl can see pretty well in the daylight. Maybe not as well as at night, but he can see well enough to outsmart that bigmouth crow, just wait and see."

Bouncer's eyes grew big for a moment until he recognized the voice of Flitter Sparrow. "Flitter!" he cried. "How nice to see you again. How long have you been sitting there?"

"Oh! Just for a few moments. It's nice to see you up

and around again, Digby. Did you sleep well?" asked the little bird.

"Yes, yes," the little groundhog nodded, "very well, thank you. By the way, Flitter, are there any of the other woodsfolk here?"

"Yes, quite a few of them. Over there at that big oak tree, the one with the big knothole in the side, you can just see Ringo Coon. In that large clump of timothy grass, a bit to the left, you can see Zippy Quail." Flitter took a big breath. "Look close at that growth of elderberry bushes by the old fence. You can just make out the tip of Dody Deer's nose peeking out. And all you have to do is sniff the wind to know that Ody Skunk is on the other side of the stream. I think Sweetie Bee, Porky Possum, Cocky Pheasant, Ziggy Snake, and Sneaky Weasel are here also, but I have not spotted them yet."

"How about Speedy Turtle and Sly Fox? Are they here?" asked Bouncer.

"Well, of course Speedy is down by the creek," the little brown bird said, "but my guess is that Sly is out somewhere getting into trouble. He's mighty good at that, you know. He even gives me a scare now and then. I just can't trust him."

"I wouldn't be surprised," Digby observed. "Wow! It looks as though most of the community has shown up for this event." At that moment, the hub-bub from the top of the pine tree grew much louder.

"Look!" someone shouted from the forest gallery. "The Professor is coming out!"

Sure enough, the pine branches at the top of the tree

suddenly exploded and from their midst shot out the figure of Professor Wiseman Owl. His bird body was somewhat larger than that of the one who had been pestering him. His wings were much fuller, wider, and longer. He did not seem to fly as fast as did Bertie Crow, but he could zoom, and swoop and dive, dip and dodge, just as well as the black bird with the big mouth. To top things off, the Professor was quite a bit smarter than the crow.

The spectators in the glade below gazed up with great interest at the air show above them. "Golly!" Bouncer exclaimed with amazement, "He does fly in the daytime! But how can he ever get away? Bertie can fly faster!"

"Just you watch," chirped Flitter, "just watch."

The wise old owl had picked his time very carefully. Bertie had just completed one of his wild, squawking dives and had zoomed well up into the air. At that instant Wiseman burst from the pine tree and went barreling away in the opposite direction. It was a moment or two before Bertie realized what had happened. By the time he could wheel about and begin the chase, Wiseman was far across the clearing and picking up speed. With a wild scream Bertie took off after the owl as fast as his feathered wings would carry him.

Digby sucked in his breath excitedly and exclaimed, "Watch out! Watch out, Wiseman! He's coming after you!" The other woodsfolk who had gathered to watch the spectacle were also shouting at the top of their voices, trying to warn the owl of the danger that was pursuing him. It was obvious to anyone watching that Professor Wiseman Owl was well liked by one and all.

"Hurry, Professor! Hurry!" squeaked Flitter Sparrow. "Hurry, Bertie is catching up!"

Bertie could fly faster than Wiseman and was catching up very fast. Just as it seemed that he was about to pounce upon his prey in mid-air, the owl slowed down suddenly and swerved sharply back across the clearing. Bertie had been flying so fast that he could not stop in time to catch the owl. He skidded through the air for quite a distance before he could gain control of himself, turn, and light out again after Wiseman.

Now Bertie, like so many other bullies, could not stand to be made to look foolish. And they don't understand that the One who made everything is not impressed by their bullying. In fact, He is very displeased with that kind of behavior. Now Bertie's anger flared even higher. He rushed after the owl, blinded by that anger. That was exactly what the Professor had counted on. His plan was going just as he had intended.

By now the spectators on the ground were wild with excitement. They cheered loudly when Bertie had been tricked by their feathered friend's plan. But now the distance between the two flying rockets above them quickly narrowed. Once again their fears for Wiseman Owl arose.

"He'll never make it!" shouted Bouncer Rabbit, as he could now see that the Professor, who was headed back toward the big pine tree, was being quickly overtaken by the crow. "He's not going to make it!"

"Oh! No!" cried Digby, "Bertie is surely going to catch Wiseman this time, and is he angry!" To everyone below it certainly appeared as though Bertie would catch up before the Professor could make it to the safety of the big pine. But just as the two flyers were almost on top of the tree, Wiseman, who everyone, including Bertie, expected to try to scramble into the thick branches, suddenly zipped straight up into the air above the tree.

Bertie Crow was not well liked by many of the woodsfolk, mainly because of his sassy, know-it-all nature. At this very moment he was absolutely certain that he had finally caught his long-time opponent. In Bertie's mind, the owl was as good as caught. That was his undoing.

Bertie didn't expect Wiseman's sudden maneuver. He was traveling so fast that he could not even begin to get stopped. As Wiseman suddenly disappeared from view, there was instantly nothing before Bertie but the big pine tree. Before he closed his eyes, everything went dark.

Digby, Bouncer, Flitter, and all the rest of the spectators were also taken by surprise. For a moment none of them could grasp what had taken place. One second it looked for certain that Bertie would slap Wiseman from the sky; the next instant, Wiseman, at the very tips of the branches of the pine tree, shot straight up toward the sun and Big Mouth Bertie Crow crashed headfirst into the thick pine branches.

Now it was true, Bertie was not too well liked, but none of the woodsfolk wanted to see him seriously hurt. At the sound of snapping, crackling branches and twigs, along with muffled crow grunts and groans, they all o-o-o-o-o-o-ed and ah-h-h-h-h-ed in unison. Then they silently held their breath. At the same time, Wiseman made a tight circle in the air, eyeing the results of his strategy.

18

For a short time it looked as though Bertie was done for. He just lay still, all tangled up in the pine limbs. "Is he dead?" It was Flitter who spoke first.

"I can't tell from here, Flitter," said Digby in a very shaky voice. "Why don't you fly up there and see?"

Before Flitter could reply, the crow and the branches began to wiggle and shake. Shortly Bertie came loose from the tangled and broken branches. Slowly he began to partly slide, partly fall from limb-tip to limb-tip, just like a big, black feathered raindrop. Shortly he fell fluttering the last few feet to the ground. He sat there for a time bobbing and blinking his eyes. The woodsfolk now rushed to the crow, concerned for his health. Suddenly they all began to talk at once. "Bertie! Bertie! Are you all right?" questioned Bouncer.

"Is he all right?" someone else asked.

"He has one eye open," replied Flitter.

"His tongue is moving," commented Porky Possum.

"Yes, yes, I think he will be all right," chattered Chatty Squirrel excitedly.

Digby moved closer to the flop-winged and badly tattered crow and inquired, "Bertie, can you say something?"

The crow shuddered and shook, bobbed and ducked, blinked and finally croaked, "Who-who put that tree up there? I-I've been sabotaged!" With that, all the woodsfolks shouted with laughter. Some rolled in the grass and laughed until animal tears streaked their faces and their sides ached. Suddenly the laughter stopped as quickly as it began. Noses began to twitch and faces changed into masks of discomfort.

A voice from the back of the crowd asked, "Is Bertie hurt?"

Heads turned for a moment, then some shouted, " Ody! It's Ody Skunk!" In an instant the clearing around the tree was empty save for Ody and Bertie.

"Are you badly hurt, Bertie?" asked the little black and white animal as she sidled up to the stunned crow. Bertie's eyes rolled wildly and he shook all over until his feathers were even more badly mussed. Once more, off in the edge of the woods, could be heard wild peals of laughter and an occasional cough as the woodsfolk made merry at the blustery crow's expense.

CHAPTER 3

Spring Storm

DIGBY AND BOUNCER slowly made their way back up the hill toward Digby's home. Along the way they talked about Bertie Crow's bad luck a short time before. Every once in a while as they talked, one or the other would bring up the sight of poor Bertie all dazed and bedraggled, and Ody Skunk rushing up to inquire after his health. Ody never was able to recognize her personal skunk effect on others at close quarters.

At the mention of the poor trapped crow with his eyes rolling and his head waggling, the two furry friends would once more go into fits of wild laughter. Finally Bouncer flopped down in the grass by the side of the trail, holding his sides and wiping away tears at the same time.

"Oh-oh! My side – Oh, if I laugh any more I will burst – Oh-oh," he groaned.

Digby leaned against an old fence post. He too was weak with laughing. After catching his breath, he said shakily, "Me too, Bounce, me too." With a few deep breaths he calmed down some and spoke once more with a more serious note in his voice. "I'm not sure we should laugh so at the bad luck of someone else. But Bertie surely did ask for all that happened to him. By the way, whatever happened to the Professor? I lost track of him in all the commotion."

Bouncer had also regained some of his self-control. He answered Digby's question soberly. "By the time that silly crow had slid to the ground, Wiseman Owl was safely perched on the very same limb from which Bertie thought he had driven him. That is one smart old bird, I must say!"

Digby, back still against the post, slid to the ground. Then he was quiet for a time and then he looked at the rabbit beside him and remarked slowly, "You know, it is a puzzle to me why the creatures must fight and squabble so much of the time. Why is it, do you suppose, that the animals, and I include Two Legs in this, are not able to live peaceably together without getting into each other's hair from time to time? I can't believe that the One who made everything wants us to be that way."

The rabbit looked very thoughtful for a time, then replied, "Beats me, Digby. You wouldn't think it was that way in the beginning. Something must have happened to cause everyone to be the way they are today. It would be so much easier if life could go along without problems and trouble."

"Bouncer, what do you suppose — I mean really suppose — it is that causes Bertie to get so upset with the Professor?"

The little rabbit shook his head and replied, "No way of knowing for sure. My guess is that it is something that comes from inside him which even he doesn't understand. Something like the thing that makes you sleep all winter, I guess. Anyway, they tell me it's been that way with crows and owls as long as anyone in the woods can remember."

The two friends sat silently resting. After a time, Digby grunted and got to his feet. "Guess we better be moving on; it's getting late," he said. "You realize this has been a very active day for me after just getting up. I will enjoy my bed very much tonight." Bouncer agreed with a nod of his head, and they began once more to amble slowly up the hill.

The following morning Digby arose from a very sound night's sleep. He tidied up his house and went out to examine the world. As usual, he first looked all around, then he sniffed the air, and after that he listened for any sound of danger. Finding none, he ventured up the hill from his house. Digby's house was located a little way up from the valley glade. Upon reaching the top, Digby stopped to gaze down upon the surrounding countryside.

To the north he could make out the outline of a farmhouse and a barn. That, he knew, was where Two Legs came from. Instinctively the little groundhog sensed that the place was full of danger. In the bright sunlight it looked pleasant, but Digby could not forget the terrible sound of that long black stick Two Legs carried with him. As well, he remembered that sometimes Two Legs brought a nasty animal with him which resembled Sly Fox. The animal was much bigger than Sly and it had a very, very ugly personality. He was vicious.

Digby was fascinated with the view of Two Legs' home. After a moment he tore his gaze away and looked off to the east toward the shiny blue ribbon far down in the valley. He had been puzzled about that ribbon ever since the first time he had come to the hilltop. The valley was full of trees, but the shiny ribbon peeked through in many places. Some of the woodsfolk said that it was like the timid brook that ran through the meadow where they lived, but much larger. "Some day," Digby said out loud, "I will go and see that thing for myself."

The groundhog's eyes traveled back across the horizon toward the west. Here was another great puzzle. Another ribbon-like figure snaked off over the distant hills. It was not bright and shiny and pretty like the one over in the east valley. This one was bluish gray and appeared to have some kind of bright stripe running down its middle. "That reminds me somewhat of Ody Skunk," he thought to himself.

What really puzzled him about the ribbon with the

stripe running down its middle was that small objects could be seen moving along on the ribbon. Yes, moving objects that looked like little bugs. Some were larger than others and they had different colors. From time to time, when the wind was blowing from that direction, Digby was almost sure that he could hear those moving bugs make a growling sound. That was odd. What kind of bugs growl?

Now Digby turned to look to the south. In that direction he was looking directly down on what he knew as his home. Not just the little knoll where his house was, but also the beautiful meadow, the cool woods, and the sparkling stream—all of it lay before his eyes and that was his home. He loved it very much. As his eyes drank in the refreshing cool green of the view down below him, a movement caught his eye.

This time of year, when the trees were putting on their new green clothes, many of the woodsfolk could be found at one time of the day or another going about the activities that made up their lives. Some of them were active in the daytime, and some were busy during the nighttime hours. In some cases, certain animals might be out and about at any hour of the day or night. Today was a typical day in Digby's community.

The movement which had caught the groundhog's eye now became more distinct. It was not a large object, nor was it bright in color. But from its actions, Digby had no trouble deciding who it was.

For a few moments the small figure would hop and flutter about in the middle of a patch of dead grass. The next moment it would dart up from the ground to the middle limbs of a nearby wild apple tree. Again one could make out a feathery motion in the midst of the apple limbs and then a small brown figure would swirl and flitter down to the patch of grass again, only to repeat the routine.

"Yes," Digby whispered to himself, "Flitter Sparrow is building her nest. Spring is truly here."

As the groundhog allowed his gaze to wander about the woodland community, he recognized many more of his friends going about their business.

In the top of the big pine tree which had been the sight of Big Mouth Bertie's downfall, he could see the motionless figure of Wiseman Owl. His daytime business was to do nothing because, in fact, the nighttime is when he makes his living.

A reddish brown movement caught Digby's attention now. It was only a flash of color in an opening in the undergrowth over where the hillside, the creek, and the woods all met. That would be Sly Fox, he knew. Sly's home was over there in the steep wall of the wooded ravine.

Digby allowed his thoughts to become words, "If Sly is up and about this early, it would be well for Bouncer Rabbit, Cocky Pheasant, Zippy Quail, and some of the other folks who appeal to Sly's taste buds, if they stay on high alert. Sly must not have found much for supper last night."

For the next few minutes, Digby continued to watch other neighbors busy with the activities of their day. Chatty Squirrel was playing a few feet off the ground on the side of a large shellbark hickory tree. She would run down the side of the tree and then suddenly stop with her head pointed toward the roots of the tree. "How can she do that?" Digby wondered to himself. "Chatty stands on the side of that tree just like I stand on the top of the hill."

Sometimes the squirrel would jump down on the ground and run about in her half hopping-half running style. When she did that, her tail rippled from bottom to top just like the little waves on the pond in the meadow when the wind blows hard. Then Chatty would scurry up the tree again and vanish from sight much like the sun when it slides out of view behind a cloud, or when it goes down behind the horizon. It was a game for her but it was also practice for one of Chatty's most important ways of protecting herself from an enemy.

On a big stump not far from Chatty's tree, a very small brown animal who was beautifully decorated with small yellow and black stripes running the length of its back, would suddenly appear and then disappear under the stump. This animal resembled Chatty Squirrel somewhat, but was much smaller and faster on its feet. In fact, many of Skippy Chipmunk's older relatives, and he too, are called "ground squirrels". Skippy was also at play among the dried leaves on the ground around the stump.

Just then another friend of Digby whizzed by his head with a very business-like sound. Digby had not heard the approach of Sweetie Honeybee until she zoomed past his ear.

"Hello, Sweetie!" exclaimed the woodchuck with joy. "It is fine to see you going about so busy. How are the flower blooms this year? Will there be a good crop of honey?"

"Oh my, yes!" replied the little yellow and black honeymaker. "It looks very good for this season. I believe this year's honey will be some of the finest. The flowers are much ahead of last year. The rains have been plentiful. In fact, we will have a big storm today. If you have any outdoor business to attend to, you better get it done soon."

Digby glanced at the sky with a doubtful eye. Above him there was nothing but blue sky. Things had cleared nicely since morning, except way off in the west he could see a small puff of a cloud just above the trees. Far above it he could see long, thin streaks of wispy clouds that reminded him of the long tail on Two Legs' horse. He had seen Two Legs riding on the horse's back one day at the edge of the meadow.

Digby declared, "I can't see anything in the sky that looks like a rain cloud. Sweetie, are you sure it's going to rain today? Don't you mean tomorrow?"

"Not at all, my friend. I mean it will rain today," buzzed the little bee, who had not stopped examining the nearby blooms during all of their conversation. "Better take my advice. Now I must get busy. I don't like flying in bad weather," Sweetie called back as she zoomed away down the hillside.

For the next half hour Digby continued to watch the activities below. It was not difficult for him to see even the smallest of his friends down there; for, you see, one thing that a groundhog most certainly has is good, keen eyesight.

Speedy Turtle could be seen sunning himself on a large rock in the middle of the clear, cool stream that wound its way through the middle of the meadow. Not far from him, on a dead log at the edge of the stream, Digby could see

Ziggy Snake also taking in the warm sunshine. And last, but not least, Cocky Pheasant could be seen stalking along in the high grass at the edge of Two Legs' last year's cornfield. From time to time Cocky's head would duck down out of sight. "He must be finding some grains of corn left on the ground from last year's crop," Digby thought to himself.

It had been some time since he had climbed to the top of the hill, and once again, the little "chuck" suddenly realized that he was terribly hungry. All about him on the crest of the hill, just waiting to be found, were tender shoots of Digby's most favorite food, clover! In a twinkling of his little black nose, he set about to fill himself. And that he did, right up to the brim of his round little woodchuck tummy. After nipping off one final sprig of clover that looked especially tasty, our furry little friend plopped himself down in the soft grass to gaze about once more.

Down below, life went on in the meadow as before. The horizon all about still showed no sign of danger from above. The sky was very bright, except that now the puffy little cloud that was far away on the horizon was larger and closer, and it had been joined by three friends. The long horse-tail clouds were now much longer and thicker. From the southeast a gentle breeze was fluttering along, moving the dead leaves around on the ground. Digby watched for a time, then his eyelids grew heavy. They fluttered a bit, opened wide, then he was asleep.

Now a nap on a sun-washed hillside with a warm south wind kissing your cheek is one of the more wonderful experiences in this world. Digby floated away on his slumber cloud. His dreams were happy scenes of all the things in life he loved the most. First came his warm winter bed, followed by good times with his friends, and then the delicious foods to be had on his hillside and in the meadow, just for the taking. His dreams were of good and joyful things.

He really had no way of knowing how long he had been asleep, and as long as those sweet dreams continued, Digby actually didn't care. In his slumber he was just in the midst of taking a large mouthful of alfalfa leaves when all of a sudden the tip of his nose turned ice cold. The new sensation caused him to jump back, thinking that some strange, icy creature had bitten his black snout. As he sat back in his dreams to ponder the mystery, two more dots of coldness plopped down on the top of his head. That sent Digby leaping to his feet, no longer sound asleep, but now wide awake. He had just returned to his senses and realized he had been dreaming, when a blinding flash of light danced all around the hilltop. At the same time, an enormous crash of sound ripped down from the sky. That noise was far worse than the sound of the black stick Two Legs carried. It caused Digby to duck his head instinctively. Something told him that the bright streak of light from the sky was the thing most to be feared.

Before the woodchuck could think anymore on the subject, he became aware that those little cold dots which had pecked his nose and head in his dreams were very real. All about him raindrops were falling faster and faster, thicker and thicker. "Oh! My goodness!" he squealed, "Sweetie was right! It is raining today – and how!"

With that he began scurrying down the hillside toward his home. Before he had gone half the distance,

Digby realized that this was the worst storm he had ever seen. The rain came down now, not just in drops, but in sheets of water through which he could hardly see to find his way. To make things worse, the gentle wind from the southeast of a few hours ago had became a raging gale. It blew so hard into his face that it seemed as though it was blowing him back up the hill.

Finally the completely soaked groundhog reached his front door and plunged inside. There he stood puffing, out of breath, and dripping wet. He shook himself until he was reasonably wrung out. To himself he thought, "That nice dry living room of mine will be most welcome – most welcome!"

Down the hallway he hurried and plunged through the living room door. He was surprised and shocked by a cold, wet feeling. With dismay Digby realized that his living room was half full of cold rain water!

CHAPTER 4

The Rescue

FOR A FEW MOMENTS Digby was so surprised to find his living room half full of cold water that he just stood there and shivered. The water was gushing into his house through the hallway that led to the back door, and it was rising fast! When the cold water rose high enough to touch Digby's tender little belly, he was shocked into action. With two big frog-like leaps he rushed back up the front hallway. For the moment again on dry ground.

Digby would find out later that he had not been nearly as careful as he should have been when he selected the spot for his back door. Even though his house was on a hillside, there were small gullies and low spots here and there, and as luck would have it, he had placed his back door in one of those little gullies. During normal rainstorms the water in the little gully did not get high enough to reach the door, but this was not a normal rainstorm! Later it would be necessary for him to do some rebuilding, but that would have to wait until the storm ended.

Digby moved back up the hallway to his front door. That door had been built in a good spot and no water was coming in. The wet groundhog crouched just inside and watched the terrible storm. There he did not get even one drop of rain on himself.

The discouraged little fellow lay still for a time, just staring out at the rain as it continued to fall in unbelievable amounts. The wind blew with a whistling rush. Between the pounding of the rain and the rushing wind, not much else captured Digby's attention. But, he had a feeling that something was trying to get through to him, and he listened closer for any sound.

At first he thought the high-pitched peeps and squeaks were just variations in the sound of the wind as it rose and fell in intensity. He was just about to forget about it when he froze in his spot and listened harder. Now he was certain that he was hearing the words, "Help! Help!

Please help! Bouncer Rabbit needs help!"

In the next moment Digby charged out into the rain. He could not see who was calling. It sounded, though, like Chatty Squirrel's voice. He headed in the direction of the meadow and Chatty's hickory nut tree home. Now a second voice joined the first. It too called frantically for help for Bouncer. Digby was certain without a doubt that it was the voice of Porky Possum. He spoke with a high-pitched drawl that was not easily mistaken.

Digby soon reached the tree, and now he could see what the problem was, even without the babbling, squealing voices and the pointing gestures of those at the scene.

The timid little stream which had always been so kind to all the woodsfolk had now been turned into an ugly, roaring river by the terrible storm which was still raging on. But that was not the major problem they faced.

Earlier that day, before the storm, Bouncer Rabbit had made his way gingerly across the stream on the pearl-like string of rocks that formed a convenient bridge. It was located well upstream from Chatty's home. The rabbit had been taken by surprise by the storm, much as Digby had been, and many others in the meadow.

Realizing too late his situation, Bouncer had tried to get back across the rock path when only the very tops of the rocks peeked through the angry waters. It took only one misstep on one of the slippery rocks and one foolish rabbit was quickly in the swift current and being swept away. Sometimes foolishness leads to placing one's feet where there is danger, as Bouncer learned in this situation.

But sometimes foolish people get lucky and get a

second chance. At just the right moment a small tree fell into the water from the strong wind, only to be seized by the raging stream and carried away. By luck the tree passed very near to the struggling rabbit. He had just enough strength left in his chilled and soaked body to squirm up onto its trunk, using one of its limbs as a handhold. Now, bumping and turning as they went, the tree and Bouncer were being swept away to wherever the stream went.

Chatty Squirrel had been playing on the side of her tree. As the first few raindrops of the storm fell before the wind and heavy rain came, she scampered up to her home high above the ground. She quickly snuggled into the knothole that formed her front door and settled down to watch the storm.

The timid little stream passed not far from Chatty's tree. Normally it was always lazy and crystal clear. Now as she watched, it first turned to a muddy brown, and then it began to rush along faster and faster, much faster than Chatty had ever seen it go. She had watched that stream most of her life. Suddenly her attention was drawn to one of the many objects that were rushing along with the water. It was a small tree in whose branches Chatty was startled to see the almost drowned figure of her friend, Bouncer Rabbit!

Chatty leaped from her doorway into the swirling wind and rain. She immediately started crying for help at the top of her squirrelly voice as she raced down the tree trunk. "Bouncer is in trouble! Help! Someone please help! Bouncer needs help!" she cried. It was that cry that roused Digby and caused him to set out to help his friend.

"Hurry!" shouted Digby as he reached the stream, "Let's try to get downstream ahead of him. Maybe we can reach him from the big rock."

Downstream from Chatty's house a very large boulder lay at what was normally the edge of the stream. But now as the group of concerned woodsfolk rushed up (many had come to help) they could see that the big rock was surrounded by swirling, muddy water.

"Oh!" cried Chatty in a sad, trembling voice, "we will never be able to get to Bouncer now!"

"Don't worry," Digby cried with false bravery, "I'm not going to see a friend lost without trying to save him. The water doesn't look too deep. And it isn't moving so swiftly here. I'm going out!"

"Be careful, Digby!" shouted a chorus of voices. "Be careful!"

Digby set off into the swirling brown water. He was able to wade to within a few feet of the rock. He then swam the rest of the distance with the familiar paddle stroke that most animals use for swimming. It looked much as though he was trying to dig a hole in the water, but it propelled him forward. In a moment he stood on the wet and very slippery rock, looking upstream for the floating tree and his friend who he was certain was very frightened.

It took only a moment for Digby to spot Bouncer and his makeshift life raft. It took just another instant for him to see that there was a very good chance for him to reach Bouncer, as there was a slight bend in the raging current that was sending floating objects like the tree in the flooded creek close by the big rock. Closer and closer the floating tree came. Digby thought to himself, "Oh! If ever you did a right thing, groundhog, do it now!"

In an instant the tree with its bedraggled passenger reached the bend in the stream and shot rapidly toward the rock. Digby braced himself as best he could on the wet boulder. As the tree approached the rock he reached down and grabbed hold of Bouncer with a clawed paw. He was just beginning to pull him up when his foot slipped on the wet rock and the startled woodchuck went headfirst into the cold, brown mass of swirling movement.

"I am going to die!" was Digby's first thought. It seemed that he had been under the water for hours, but really it was only for an instant. As his head broke through the surface of the water into the fresh, wet air, he too, as had Bouncer, had a stroke of luck. He was within reach of the floating tree. Grabbing hold of it he pulled himself aboard. As the cries of the woodland folk still on the shore faded into the distance, Digby and Bouncer were swept away on their tree raft in the raging water.

For the first few minutes after pulling himself onto the lifesaving tree, Digby clung tightly to its limbs. He feared that if he moved it would tip over, spilling its cargo into the roily flood. When that did not happen, he finally mustered up enough courage to open one eye. What he saw caused him to pop the other eye open quickly. About him, Digby could see that the stream had grown much wider. And now it was passing through a strange countryside. Strange, that is, only because Digby had never seen it before. At first he was terribly frightened, but after a time he began to feel that the tree was much more steady in the water than he first supposed. And, the countryside could offer little danger as long as they were in the middle of the stream. He relaxed a little, but still he knew that there was great danger right where they were.

A sudden thought exploded inside his brain. It startled him so badly to instantly remember that in all the excitement he had forgotten his friend. "BOUNCER!" he screeched at the top of his lungs. "BOUNCER! Where are you?"

A weak and quavery voice came from behind him. "Here—here, Digby! Here I am. NO! No! Don't move around so much!" he squealed as Digby tried to turn around enough to look at the waterlogged rabbit behind him. "You'll upset the tree! Just s-i-t still!"

Digby stopped moving about so much because he knew his friend was badly frightened. He also knew that none of Bouncer's family had ever been blessed with a great degree of courage. This present member of the cottontail clan was no different. Their greatest defense against danger was to run away. Bouncer was a runner, not a fighter.

The groundhog moved again, but this time much more slowly. He inched himself around until he was able to see Bouncer behind him. For a time they looked at each other with sad eyes. Then a very weird thing happened. Digby began to laugh. Slowly at first, then he burst out with very long, loud guffaws. Bouncer was taken aback for a moment, then he too broke out into peals of laughter.

Now two almost drowned animals clinging to a floating tree being swept down a raging stream while at the same time laughing wildly makes little sense. Maybe it was caused by the nervous strain of the moment. But more so, it was caused by what each one saw when he looked closely at the other one. Whatever the cause, it may have been the best thing that could have happened. At least for the moment, the strain was released and they could think a bit more clearly.

When Digby first looked back and got a glimpse of Bouncer, he saw what looked like a soggy, gray ball wrapped so tightly around one of the tree's limbs that at first it looked like just a fat spot on the limb. One thing that told him it was not a tree limb with a fat spot was two big fear-rounded rabbit eyes peering at him from that odd-looking bump. It was indeed Bouncer Rabbit, and the sight of him set Digby off into wild laughter.

Bouncer took a closer look at the groundhog when he saw him break into wild guffaws. In that moment he had the thought that Digby looked like a spongy chunk of an old log that had been laying on the forest floor for too many years. When that "chunk of log" wiggled and squirmed, trying to find a more comfortable seat on the tree trunk, Bouncer couldn't hold back. At a sight like that, he too let go his mirth in high-pitched squeaky giggles. That is the way it is with young lives. Many times they do not take danger as seriously as they should. Digby and Bouncer were still in a serious situation.

Bouncer's face became more serious now. "Where do you think we are by now?" His tone of voice showed his concern. About them the stream had grown even more wild and raging.

"No way of telling. This is completely strange country

to me," the woodchuck replied. "All we can do now is go where this tree goes. It will be getting dark soon and we will have to be careful not to go to sleep or we might fall off this tree."

"J-J-Just now, I-I-I think that is the l-least of our w-worries! LOOK THERE!" Bouncer's voice quavered and then rose into almost hysterical fear. "OH! OH! Digby! What is that?"

"GOODNESS! Oh! Goodness! I can't tell you what it is, but hold on tight – HERE WE GO-O-O--O-O-o-o-o-o-o!" Digby cried out, his words being lost in the rushing sounds as the tree and its terrified cargo were swept away now, faster and faster by a great new flood of water.

The new wildly cascading body of water that now held them captive kept them in its grip for almost an hour. They were propelled along at a much faster speed than before. From time to time the tree bumped and jolted as it hit things under the surface of the water or was struck by other floating objects. It took all the strength Digby and Bouncer had just to hold onto their seats in the tree. It may have been a bit easier for Digby than Bouncer because, you see, groundhogs do climb trees at times. A rabbit's paws are made for hopping and running, not climbing.

After a time neither of the two castaways spoke. It was just easier to hold tightly and think about better times. Digby was doing that very thing when their wild journey was abruptly interrupted. With memories of his grass-covered hill all bristled with new-grown clover and alfalfa sprigs, flowers, and sunshine, he was paying little attention to the way ahead. He never saw the small waterfall over which the tree was catapulted.

For a moment the sensation of falling blotted out all other thoughts and fears. Then, rather than the expected chilling bath in the cold waters, a sudden bone-jarring jolt shook his grip loose from the tree limb. Lo and behold, the next moment he was tumbling into a pile of water-smoothed boulders. He no sooner came to a stop when a small, wet, furry rabbit came crashing down on top of Digby's stomach. Nevertheless, after catching their breath, which had been knocked out of both of them, they sat up and realized that by some miracle they were on reasonably dry land. Digby said out loud, "Whoever the great power is that made this miracle happen, we need to thank Him."

It was practically dark now. The two lost travelers huddled together for warmth. Even that was not enough to keep their teeth from chattering. It was only early springtime and the nights still became quite chilly.

"M-m-m-m-my but it is cold!" Bouncer quavered. "The water sounds so c-c-c-close. Maybe it's g-g-g-getting c-c-c-c-closer."

"N-n-n-now d-d-don't let y-y-your imagination run away, Bouncer," the groundhog chattered through his teeth. "It w-w-will be warmer when the s-s-s-sun c-c-c-comes up."

"Yes, I-I-I know, Digby. Thank you for rescuing me." Bouncer's voice faded. Digby chuckled to himself, thinking that both the one to be rescued and the rescuer both need rescuing now. He grunted a couple of times, then both soon fell into a troubled sleep. They were completely unaware that two pairs of eyes stared out across the water at them on the small spot of dry land, where the two lost ones slept.

Those two pairs of eyes had followed Digby and Bouncer for a great part of their journey. Little did they know that the next morning, when the sun came up, a very unexpected welcome awaited them.

CHAPTER 5

Digby Meets Himself
on the Way Home

IT WAS A VERY cold and uncomfortable night. The little groundhog roused from his fitful sleep many times only to doze off again. Now he woke once more. This time it was to a chilly gray world rather than the wet, dark one of the night. For a short time he could not get his mind to understand just what had happened. Through the grayness, a slight feeling of warmth could be felt. In the east the sky was brightening with a rising sun. The sound of running water was still close by, but somehow things seemed different.

"Bouncer! Bouncer!" he called out. "Bouncer! Are you awake?"

"M-M-m-m-m- yes, I think so but – SAY! Why can't I see anything? I'm sure my eyes are open, but I can't see a thing!" Bouncer squealed in a panicked voice. "Digby! Why can't I see?"

"Easy, Bouncer," Digby replied, fully aware of the rabbit's timid nature. "I think it's only the thick fog. Don't get upset. When it clears I think we will be able to see and maybe we can tell then how bad our situation is."

"Fog! Only fog! Oh! Thank the Good One who made all things. It's only fog. I thought I had lost my eyesight in all that terrible experience," jabbered the emotional little rabbit. A little more settled now, he continued, "Digby, do you remember what happened last night at all?"

"Yes, I guess so. At least most of it," came the reply.

"Do you remember what I said to you just before we went to sleep?" the rabbit continued in a warm, soft voice.

Digby answered through the fog in a rather embarrassed tone. "Well-l-l-l, yes, most of it I guess. But maybe not all of it."

"I said, thank you for rescuing me, Digby. Thank you!" The rabbit stated his words in a very positive manner.

Nothing was said for a time between the two fogbound friends. Finally Digby replied in an apparently confused state of mind. "Bouncer, I don't understand what you mean. I didn't rescue you. We both ended up in the river and now we both will have to be rescued."

"That's not what I meant," Bouncer came back. "I know if you hadn't been on this journey with me that I wouldn't have had the courage to hold on all the way down the river. Yes—yes, you did. You are the best kind of friend, Digby, the kind who gives strength to others. Thank you again!"

Digby didn't say anything for quite a while. He just sat considering what Bouncer had said. He gave it much thought then thought to himself, "I sure think a lot of this poor, scared little fellow. Somehow I have to get him out of this mess and back home."

The two did not have long to wait before it became obvious that their luck had changed. The fog began to lift as the heat of the sun increased. Off to the right of what had been their little island last night, where they had landed with a jolt, Digby could see a narrow band of solid ground running from where they rested over to the shore. Though the muddy river water still ran swiftly, it had gone down just enough to reveal a path of escape for them.

"BOUNCER! LOOK!" Digby shouted. "Come on, we're free! WE ARE FREE!" Certainly for anyone who has ever been trapped by some evil thing, finding a way to freedom is a feeling hard to describe. The two friends now knew that feeling.

The groundhog's violent outburst came so suddenly that the rabbit crouched down instinctively in fear. Then, realizing what Digby had shouted, he too charged off after the groundhog, who was by now making his way across the muddy sandbar towards the shore.

Unknowingly, the two friends were rushing straight toward the spot on the shore from where the two pairs of curious eyes had peered at them while they slept. They had kept watch over the island all during the night. Even now those eyes were watching the muddy parade across the sandbar as Bouncer and Digby sloshed and slipped on their way to the riverbank.

Digby had reached a point about ten feet from the shore when he pulled up to an abrupt stop and stood on his hind legs. Oh, yes, groundhogs can stand on their hind legs when they want to. His stopping was so sudden that Bouncer, who had been struggling along through the misty dawn light, did not stop in time and ran his nose right into the middle of Digby's back. That jarring contact caused the rabbit to lose his footing on the narrow slice of land. Into the cold water his back legs and tail went.

"OH! OH! Not again! My tail will never get dried out at this rate. I'll be the only rabbit in the forest with mildew on my tail!" wailed Bouncer. "Digby! What on earth are you doing?"

Bouncer dragged himself back onto the spit of land and started to dry himself off. Suddenly, out of the mist, came a black shape swooping and squalling above them. The rabbit was so stunned that he nearly fell back into the river. Neither of them could grasp what was happening, and Bouncer cried out for Digby.

The woodchuck, at that moment, could also make out more clearly a large, brown object standing on the riverbank.

That is what had caused him to stop so abruptly. Suddenly, with a shout of joy, Digby scrambled up the incline as fast as his short woodchuck legs could take him. "Dody! – Bertie! Bouncer! It's Dody and Bertie! We are really rescued now," he yelled back to his friend.

"Dody Deer! – Bertie Crow! – How did you find us?" Bouncer squealed as he bounded up onto the shore and began to dance about with the others. "How in the world did you find us?"

"What do you mean, 'find you?' We never lost you," cawed Bertie. "We never lost you!"

Both Digby and Bouncer who made it on shore, stared at Bertie in disbelief. "What do you mean?" asked Digby.

"Well," began Dody in her soft, quiet voice, "when the alarm went out through the community that you two had been swept away, Bertie and I both started out after you. You see, it is nothing for Bertie to fly over miles of this valley. And I have traveled this far down the river and even farther many times. We have been beside you and above you all the way down here. Out there in the river, though, you couldn't hear us call to you."

"That's right, I flew just above your heads many times, but the roar of the river was too much for you to hear me," Bertie chimed in. "When we saw you go over the falls, we decided to wait until this morning. We were hoping we could find some way of rescuing you from your island. Luckily the water level dropped during the night and that strip of land made a path for you. All we had to do then was wait for you," he explained.

"Now we are going to lead you home. It will not be

an easy trip. There are some dangers but we will make it back. It will take much more time than it did coming down, though," Dody advised them with quiet assurance.

"We don't know how to thank the two of you," Digby exclaimed with a serious note in his voice. "I guess we don't really appreciate our friends until they do something really wonderful for us. Wouldn't it be great if everyone in the world could be friends?"

"Look who is talking!" squawked Bertie, "Wasn't it you who did that very thing for Bouncer here?"

"Yes, he certainly did," Bouncer exclaimed. Then another thought came into his head and he continued, "There is one other thing that needs to be cleared up and made right. Bertie, we owe you an apology for the way we laughed at you the other day when you had your troubles with the Professor and then Ody Skunk. I, for one, am very sorry, and I'm sure Digby is too."

"Forget it, I probably had it coming," the embarrassed crow mumbled. "You keep that up and you will be the first person to see a black crow blush red."

Everyone laughed with Bertie as he made light of himself. Their laughter relaxed all of them. The discomfort and hardships of the previous day and night were quickly being forgotten. The happiness of good friendship was taking hold of their spirits. Now it was time to start the long journey home.

The first few hours of the return trip were easy. The countryside along the river was flat for quite a distance on either side. When the little group finally reached the place where their timid little brook emptied into the big river, the going became much more difficult because the lay of the land through which the brook flowed was much rougher. After about an hour of difficult travel, Digby and Bouncer begged for a rest stop.

"Whew!" exploded Digby, "I'm bushed! Let's stop for a while and rest."

"Yes! Oh yes," echoed Bouncer. "My legs feel like weeping willow branches wobbling around in a high wind. Let's rest!"

"All right," agreed Dody, "we might as well. We will have to stop quite a few times before we get back to the meadow. It's not difficult for me because my legs are much longer. And Bertie can soar on the wind without much effort. But you two little fellows can't cover as much distance as we can without rest. Just stop us any time you feel like it."

Bertie came swirling down from the clear sky above to land beside the resting group. "Everybody worn out?" piped the talkative crow. "We'll take it easy. We have a goodly distance to travel. Now for me it would be much less than an hour's trip. But then you know that I go as the crow flies. For you it will be more than a day yet before you get home at the speed you can travel."

"I just got through telling all that, Bertie," Dody said accusingly. "And by the way, you are not the only one who could make that trip in a short time. Our job is to get these two home, not brag on how quickly we can make the trip."

Bertie hung his head and looked away. "I'm sorry," he said with embarrassment. "I guess I've just got a big mouth! Somehow I have to learn how to get control of my tongue so I don't make other people uncomfortable."

51

Digby and Bouncer glanced at each other with a glint in their eyes and sly smiles, but they did not let Bertie see.

"Dody," Digby spoke up, "yesterday, as I was at the top of my hill, I could look down this valley and see a beautiful silver ribbon here among the trees. I told myself that I would come and see it someday. But when I got here, all I saw was a muddy brown river. Why is that? Can you tell me why I did not find a silver ribbon?"

"Digby, sometimes the beautiful things we see in the distance are not nearly as beautiful as we think once we get near them," Dody replied with a knowing answer. "Also, there are beautiful things that are made ugly by things that are evil. It would be best for all of us in our lives to stay away from evil things and try to be as beautiful inside as we can be. My friend, the river is normally beautiful, but the evil of the storm filled it with mud and trash and made it ugly."

"You mean then, that my silver ribbon became that muddy river?" Digby asked in awe.

"Yes, it did," Dody replied, "but don't be disappointed, little woodchuck; many things, unhappily, are that way in this world. Take my advice. Look ahead only as far as you can clearly see, but never stop looking that far."

Bouncer, who had been listening intently, spoke up now. "Hey! Look, you two, that's getting pretty deep. Anyway, we have rested long enough. Let's get on our way. I want to get back home."

"Let's talk again, Dody," Digby said quietly as they rose to continue their trip. "I really like to listen to the things you say. I never knew these things mean that much."

"Yes, Digby, anytime you wish," Dody replied with her quiet smile, "anytime."

Once again the four travelers made their way slowly along the twisting, turning little brook with its crooked little pathway that would soon bring them home, but not before Digby would learn something about himself which he had not known before.

Evening came after a hard day of walking. After nibbling some sweet clovers for supper, Digby and his friends made their beds and fell quickly asleep. Bertie had found a large limb of an oak tree which suited him perfectly as a bed. Dody had made her way into a brushy thicket for the night, while Digby and Bouncer had found a cozy nook beneath the arched roots of Bertie's oak tree. There would be no dreams tonight. Each of the travelers were more than weary enough to sleep soundly all night long.

Dawn had come and gone and the warm morning sun was looking down among the trees when Dody and Bertie roused their small friends. They had allowed the two little fellows to sleep an extra hour. They knew that the frightening ride down the flooded river and now the long walk home had drained their strength. But, now it was time to move on.

After waking up, the two sleepyheads spent some time stretching and yawning, then they ate some clovers and did quite a bit of mumbling about how early it was. Then the small caravan set out once more.

As they made their way beside the brook, Bouncer began to perk up. Soon he kicked his heels into the air and sped away ahead of Dody and Digby. Bertie circled above them.

"Well, it looks as though our cotton-tailed friend has returned to his old self," Dody observed. "He must have gotten his spirits dried out too."

Digby chuckled his groundhog giggle in agreement, "Yes, I guess so. You know, that rabbit is my best friend, but I don't really know why." He studied a bit and continued, "Dody, I'm not even sure I completely know what friendship is."

Dody looked at the woodchuck with smiling eyes as he plodded along beside her. Then she spoke slowly, "Digby, I believe sincerely that if and when we are able to explain friendship completely with words, we very possibly don't have true friendship. I believe that true friendship is like that thing we call love. It goes far beyond the meanings of words. It is something we give and receive, feel and experience, without ever being able to draw lines around it." With that Dody grew silent.

"Dody," Digby sighed, "I never have thought about it like you do. Don't stop talking. Tell me more of it. More of how you feel about serious things. Please don't stop."

Dody roused up and began speaking again. "I just can't turn it on and off like the rain. Those thoughts only come when something happens to make me stop and think deeply. As you live and learn of life it will be the same for you. One day you too will be able to put the pieces of life into thoughts which will allow you to live that life."

"My, oh my, that's just beautiful, Dody." With that Digby turned his attention to one problem that had bothered him at times as long as he could remember. HE WAS HUNGRY!

The four travelers stopped for lunch. It was either that or have poor Digby faint dead away with hunger, or so he thought. Bertie was pecking away at various wild seeds. Dody found some tender leaves to her liking. Digby and Bouncer feasted on sweet grasses which they enjoyed so much. But this was a time of great danger. Anytime animals are feeding they are very open to enemies.

Not one of the four heard, smelled, or saw the coming attack until it was upon them. Each reacted instinctively.

Bertie squawked and leaped into the air in an embarrassingly awkward manner. In doing so he left two or three of his tail feathers fluttering in the breeze. He was the first to be attacked. In just a matter of moments he was circling well above the treetops. It was his warning that alerted the others.

Dody did instantly what her instinct's voice told her to do. Her head and tail both came up at the same time. Dody's tail looked like what Two Legs would call a white "flag". She also snorted a loud "huffing" sound which all deer do when startled. It was only a matter of seconds and she was gone from sight. She sprang away with huge, bounding leaps. Dody's first and greatest defense against danger is her ability to run very fast.

Bouncer did much the same as Dody Deer. A rabbit's instinct in reaction to danger is also to run. Whereas Dody streaked away through the woodlands, Bouncer zig-zagged off toward the nearest briar patch, which happened in this case to be just at the edge of the clearing where moments before they all had been enjoying dinner. Now, from his hiding place, Bouncer was able to clearly see the rest of the episode. Digby C. Groundhog was about to come face to face with a side of himself which he never knew of in the past.

At the moment when Bertie let go with his ear-shattering squawk of alarm in response to the unannounced attack, Digby had just filled his mouth with juicy greenery. The sudden outburst, Dody's dash for safety, and Bouncer's scamper to the briar patch caused Digby to delay any attempt to escape for an instant. That was simply due to curiosity over the uproar, which can be a fatal mistake at times.

Then the realization of nearby danger caused the groundhog to swallow his food in one gulp. He began to gallop about looking for a place to hide, a hole in the ground, a tree, anything! Then, finding none close enough, Digby stopped in the middle of the clearing and reared up on his hind legs.

The groundhog's sharp teeth showed now in a vicious smile-like grimace. From his throat came a snarling growl which he never before knew he could make. The hair on his back stood up brush-like and he felt a strange hot feeling of something completely unlike the feelings of love, friendship, and happiness he usually had. That hot feeling streaked through him. For the first time in his life Digby was ready to defend himself.

Now in front of him the danger stood. Facing Digby stood a dog, something like the one that usually travels with Two Legs, but this one was much smaller. It was light brown in color with some white spots and it had a very bushy tail. The dog also showed his sharp white teeth in a nasty smile. From its throat came an angry growl. Once more, as for countless times in the past, two animals stood on the brink of combat. They never know why other than to obey the tiny voice of instinct speaking from within.

Bouncer, watching from the briar patch, was simply terrified. His heart beat terribly fast. He wanted to call out for his friend to run to safety but his voice would not come. All he could do was watch. As he did so, he saw the dog make a sudden lunge toward Digby. To his total amazement he saw the dog recoil backwards with Digby firmly attached to his nose. The dog let go a yelp of pain and a defeated cry, "LET GO MY NOSE! – OH! PLEASE LET GO!"

Digby let go his mouthful of dog nose and scuttled back to his position of defiance. The dog circled him once, then Digby made another quick move to attack. At that the dog turned and tore off though the woods as fast as he could go, still yelping now and then, and stopping often to rub his nose in the grass. The battle was done. Digby had won, which surprised him as much as anybody.

When the other travelers recovered from their stunned amazement and realized that Digby stood victorious, they rushed to his side. They shouted and danced and laughed for joy. Dody returned shortly to be told by an excited crow and rabbit how Digby had defeated the dog. Then the gentle deer turned to the woodchuck and quietly said, "That is another part of friendship that I didn't mention; standing up for your friends against danger."

Digby was slumped on the ground by now in trembling exhaustion. He looked up at those big, brown, gentle eyes of the deer and mumbled, "I'm not sure I even thought about what I was doing at the time, Dody. It just seemed to happen as though it was the thing I had to do. I do know one thing. I did not enjoy the way I felt when I was so terribly angry, but I was scared at the same time. It seemed to be the only thing I could do. That dog would not stop bothering me. I think he wanted to kill me. And besides, I did not enjoy seeing Bertie's tail feathers torn out either!"

At that remark the crow's eyes grew big, very big, with a pained look. His head spun around toward his rear flying equipment. He began to wail and hop about, crying, "MY TAIL FEATHERS! Oh, my beautiful, black tail feathers! How could that terrible dog do such a thing? I wonder how he would like it I were to sneak up behind him and pull all the hairs out of his tail? Oh! Oh!"

It was hard for the others not to laugh at the wailing crow. So they busied themselves with finishing their interrupted meal. They had to have strength to finish their journey. After that, they settled down for a good night's rest.

The next morning found the party of travelers on the trail early. Before the sun reached the center of the sky overhead, a call of joy came down from Bertie Crow, "Digby, I can see your hillside! We're almost home!" Off he swooped to spread the news to the Friendship Meadow community. In a few short minutes Digby and Bouncer were making their way across the stone pearl bridge. By now the shiny brook was almost back to normal.

On the other side of the stream the woodland community of woodsfolk was shouting with their happiness at the return of the lost ones. Everyone was so overtaken with the joyous occasion that not even one person objected when Ody Skunk, perfume and all, ambled up to the weary travelers with tears of happiness streaming down her striped face. She wailed, "Oh! You poor lost boys, come here and let me give you a big hug."

All were happy because the lost had been saved and there was great joy in the community of friendship and happiness.

CHAPTER 6

Stranger on the Meadow

THE GRAND HOMECOMING festivities were over. The community had been caught up in a happy uproar late into the night. By the time the party had ended, Digby was too tired to make the climb up to his hillside home, so he and Bouncer just curled up beneath the roots of Chatty Squirrel's tree and spent the night much as they had on their long journey home.

The next morning, not very early, the two young friends awoke, had breakfast, and parted to go to their separate homes. On the walk up to his home, it dawned on Digby that he might have to look for a new homesite. He remembered that the last time he was in his house, his living room was half full of cold rain water.

When he got to his front door, the groundhog stood looking around a moment then entered in. First he made his way to his living room. There he was greeted with a sad sight. The water had disappeared, but there was a thick layer of goopy mud all over the floor and halfway up the walls. He looked at the mess for a moment, then he turned and walked out, taking nothing with him. You see, groundhogs don't worry about owning things.

Digby made his way to the back door of his house. There he found the source of the problem. Under normal conditions his selection of a site for the door was good, but when a storm came of the size of the one a few days before, it was not acceptable. Then the water came rushing too fast and too high and ran into Digby's house, down the back hallway, and into his living room. There was no need to go farther, he would have to build a new home.

"My! It's warm for this kind of work," Digby mumbled to himself as he stood back and viewed his labor. The woodchuck had been at work for two days. The front door and hallway of his new house were done and he was just about to begin work on his new living room.

He had been careful in choosing his new homesite.

It was not far from his old house. This time he had chosen wisely the location of both front and back doors. Digby loved his hillside, so it was not unexpected that he would locate his new home not far from the old one.

The little chuck had been digging steadily for much of the morning—digging and shoving dirt up the hallway and out the door. After hours of digging and shoving, digging and shoving, he finally flopped down in a heap of exhaustion. Then, after a long rest, he decided to go back to work again. "Up, boy," he urged himself, "up and at it. No one else is going to build your house for you, you know, so get busy."

The groundhog stood up, moved a bit closer to the wall of earth in front of him, and dug into it with both paws. He made only a few swipes in the solid dirt when his paws struck something much harder than dirt. He jerked back his smarting paw with a loud, "Ow-w-w-w!" He hopped about for a while with his paw jammed into his mouth.

When groundhogs dig, it is not unusual for them to run into rocks now and then as they work. Generally they are able to dig them loose and push them out of the way with the rest of the "diggins". This time though, Digby was not to be so lucky. After his bruised paw had stopped hurting, he set about to explore the obstacle which was before him. In a short time he could see that it was no small pebble lying in his way. Instead, it was a quite large boulder. He was certain that even if he could dig it loose, he would not be able to push the heavy rock up the hallway and out the door. What he was to do now he just didn't know.

In another part of the meadow, Sly Fox had spent a

bad night. He had set out to find an evening meal about an hour after the large springtime moon had risen. He had searched about for quite a while looking for Ziggy Quail's nest. He knew he might find newly laid eggs there. Quail eggs always made a good meal. But Sly's luck was not too good, or else Ziggy's choice of a nest site was extra good this year. The sinister fox just couldn't find the prize he was looking for.

After dropping his search for quail eggs, Sly decided to head over toward Two Legs' farm. He now had visions of a nice fat chicken for supper. It had been a long time since he had tasted chicken. He knew, though, that it was a dangerous trip. The last time he went there he had been interrupted right at the chicken yard fence by Two Legs' dog. Right after that came a great booming roar from Two Legs' stick. But even at that, Sly was willing to take the risk. A fox has to eat, doesn't he? He would have a great feast if he was successful, so off he loped in the direction of Two Legs' farm.

Sly had reached the crest of the hill above the farm lot and was gazing down upon the chicken yard with great anticipation. Suddenly, from not far behind him, he heard a sound which sent prickles of fear up and down his spine. Not waiting for the sound to come a second time, Sly set off toward the east at a mile-eating gallop. Not far behind him came the wavering howl that he had just heard. It rose and wavered with a blood-curdling wail.

Sly Fox had experienced this kind of thing a number of times before. The wavering call behind him was that of a dog. Two Legs' dog, to be exact. He was a hunting dog whose nose was very keen and able to follow the fox. His melodious wail told his master that the fox was running and in what direction. All Sly could do was growl to himself, "Oh! No! Not again. Well, unless I can get that blabber-mouthed dog off my trail there will be no supper for me tonight." And on he ran.

Sly had no luck losing the dog. The chase lasted much of the night and it covered many miles. Sly had tried just about every trick he knew to fool that dog. He crossed and recrossed every little stream he came to. He ran along fallen logs, jumping from one to another. He doubled back on his own tracks then leaped to a nearby rock, but nothing worked.

"That is one smart blabber-mouthed dog," he grumbled through panting breath. "I started out to hunt tonight and now I'm the one being hunted – blabber-mouthed dog!"

After trying all his tricks and failing to fool the dog, it was by accident that Sly lost his pursuer. He had been running mostly through the woods and rough country during the chase. Now he came upon a large open field surrounded by a fence. Sly decided to give it a try since nothing else had worked. So under the fence he slithered and across the moonlit field he sped. As he approached the middle of the field a group of large, dark, moving objects suddenly loomed in front of him. Sly made no effort to avoid the group. At his speed he was in and out of their midst in a flash. There was a sudden snorting and pawing of sharp hoofs. He could hear the running footsteps for a short time and then he ran in silence. He also could no longer hear the "Ow-w-w-w, ow-w-w-w" of the dog either.

Now Sly could slow down to a restful trot.

What the fox could not know was that because he had accidentally run through a herd of cows, the dog lost his trail. For some reason, many dogs can seldom follow a track where cows have just walked. The odor of the cow must somehow plug up the dog's nose worse than a summer cold. And so it was that Sly fox got away for that time.

Now it was past sunup the next morning. Sly was loping along just at the edge of the woodland community. He was only now returning from his long run of the night before and he was still hungry. The wily fox glanced left and right. Nothing escaped his sharp eyes. Suddenly, up ahead in some high grass, a patch of gray bobbed among the green blades. It took Sly only a moment to recognize the light summer coat of Bouncer Rabbit. And only another moment to decide that a fine meal lay just ahead of him.

There was no hunting involved now. It was just a burst of blinding speed which carried the fox to the rabbit in a flash. Bouncer never saw Sly coming. It was just by luck that the browsing rabbit bent down to get another mouthful of juicy clover. It was that movement that caused Sly to miss his mark, and it allowed Bouncer the small amount of time necessary to make a dash for safety. And that he did!

Bouncer had been eating not far from his house. The instant he realized the great danger he was in, the little rabbit sped off toward the safety of his humble home. It was humble because Bouncer had taken it over from a previous occupant who had left it long ago. It wasn't fancy but it served him well.

The rabbit's crazy zig-zag manner of running was very

difficult for the larger fox to follow. But Sly was not about to give up. Closer and closer he came to the bobbing white tail of the terrified rabbit. A time or two the snapping of fox teeth close behind that white spot caused Bouncer to run all the faster. He put forth a greater burst of speed which kept him just beyond the wickedly grinning snout of the hungry fox.

Up ahead Bouncer could see his front door come into view. A few more leaps and he would be safe. That ray of hope caused him to cry out to himself, "RUN! YOU DUMB RABBIT, RUN!"

At his very door the rabbit could feel the hot breath of the fox on his tailend. With one last great leap, Bouncer plunged down the front hallway of his house, safe now from Sly Fox for the moment, but right into a most startling experience.

Bouncer's house had been built much like Digby's house. As Bouncer dived down his front hallway, he fully expected to land on its rough, stony floor. But instead, much to his surprise, he landed on what was for just a moment a soft, warm, furry pillow. The next instant, though, that soft pillow exploded into a wild ball of ferocious snarling action.

The rabbit somehow catapulted on past whatever that growling, snarling mass of energy was, and landed at the door to his sleeping room. Above him in the hallway, the ruckus was deafening. Bouncer could in no way tell what was happening. All he knew was that he was too exhausted to go farther. He just flopped down and waited for what he thought was going to be the end of him. "My goodness!

Oh, my goodness!" he wailed. "What did I do to deserve all of this?"

Sly Fox's long run of the night before had reduced his energy just enough so that he couldn't quite catch that slippery rabbit. The rabbit popped into his hole and Sly was going after him. You see, the fox is a good digger like many other animals. He had just poked his nose into Bouncer's front door when it seemed as though the very inside of the earth exploded in his face. From within the rabbit hole came the most blood-curdling bellow Sly had ever heard. Right behind that sound came a ball of fury the likes of which the fox had never faced.

Now foxes are known for their slyness and in certain cases they can be very dangerous fighters. But at this moment Sly's fighting ability was of no use. In a matter of seconds the animal that boiled from Bouncer's house was all over the fox like a swarm of angry bees. Bites and scrapes, kicks and more bites covered Sly like a blanket, and this stranger was strong, very strong! The fox struggled but could not break free from his opponent's grip for a long while. Finally, with one great lunge, Sly tore himself loose. Down the trail he fled, howling and yowling all the way at the top of his lungs. "Ow-w-w-w ouch-o-o-o, stay away from me! Someone keep that thing away from me! Ow-w-w-w-!" Sly Fox had forgotten all about being hungry.

The silence after the battle almost hurt Bouncer's ears. His heart beat so hard he thought it would wear a hole in his chest. He had regained some of his breath by now. After thinking about it for a moment, he decided it would be a good idea for him to slip out his back door. He certainly didn't want to face whatever that thing was at his front door.

The rabbit quietly slipped out the back door and made his way around some low brush beneath which his house lay. He peeked around a tree warily. There, crouched at his front door, he could see an animal of a kind he had never seen before. At first he thought it was one of Digby's older brothers. But after a second look, he could tell that there could only be a distant family connection, if any.

The stranger was built low and somewhat squatty. He had a very strong-looking body. He was somewhat bigger than Digby, quite a bit in fact. His coat was not a solid color, but instead it was streaked with whitish stripes across his peppery gray body. Bouncer could see a pair of dark eyes peering all about. The defiant glint in those eyes caused the timid hare to shudder with fear.

Bouncer was torn between that fear and a feeling of anger at having some stranger simply walk in and take over his home. After debating it in his mind for a bit, he decided to make whatever protest a weak little rabbit could make.

Bouncer's first move was to pick a spot in the bushes directly in front of his front door which provided a safe place from where he could make his protest. Picking just the right time when the stranger was looking away, he bounded away through the undergrowth. In a moment he was nestled in the protected place he had picked.

The stranger's head flew around when he heard the rustling of the leaves and twigs from Bouncer's running feet. He was not able to spot the speedy hare, but his very nature caused him to charge out toward the sound regardless of what had caused it. Not being able to pinpoint exactly where Bouncer was hiding, the angry animal stopped a few yards from Bouncer's house. There he snarled out a challenge to the source of the sound.

"You! Whoever you are, come out and face me!" the stranger bellowed. At that, Bouncer closed his eyes and hugged the earth tightly. He felt sure he was going to faint and fall right over.

"Hey, you! Come out or I'm coming in!" The challenge was now a fearful bellow. There was silence again as the rabbit's jaws were locked shut with terror. For the third time the newcomer shouted, "COME OUT, I SAY!"

Bouncer finally mustered up what little courage he had. He knew he had to do something to try and recover his home. "You were digging in my home, sir," he finally managed to squeak out.

The frailty of the voice from the bushes seemed to calm the stranger some. His voice came again, loud, but without such a vicious tone to it. "Who are you - speak up," he said.

"It's just me," quavered the rabbit.

"Who is 'me'?" came an impatient reply.

"B-B-B-ouncer R-Rabbit," came the quavering reply.

"Ho-ho! A rabbit!" In a moment the attitude of the stranger changed and he seemed just about to become relaxed. Then he went on, "What do you mean, your house? It's only your house if you can keep it and that you don't seem to be able to do! Ha-ha."

At that moment the teasing laughter stopped abruptly as a voice from behind the stranger caused him to quickly assume a position that left no doubt that he was ready to do battle.

"We might also ask who you are. And what makes you think you can just walk in and steal someone else's home?" Digby Groundhog said in an even voice. He stood just in front of Bouncer's front door. Though he showed no outward signs of being ready to fight, the look on his face and the coolness of his voice left no one present in doubt of his intentions.

"Who's asking?" came the sassy voice of the newcomer. "Just who's asking?"

"Digby C. Groundhog."

"And what is this to you?"

"The rabbit is my friend."

"And what are you going to do about it?"

"That depends on you. Again, sir, what is your name?"

"Toughy Badger, if you must know!"

"Well, Mr. Badger, I would like to see this settled without trouble. But since the rabbit is my friend, and since he is not equipped to defend himself, I guess I would have to meet you face to face," Digby replied coolly.

"YOU! Face me? Ha-ha! Look groundhog, don't you know that I am one of the best fighters in all of the animal world? You wouldn't stand a chance against me!" boasted the badger.

"That all may be," replied the chuck. "I have heard Professor Owl tell of your family's fighting history. Most likely you can defeat me. Nevertheless, I would have to face you."

At that moment, from the east side of the clearing,

another voice joined the conversation. "Mr. Badger, I'll help Digby against you, and I am also one of the better fighters around." It was the voice of Ringo Coon.

Ringo had no sooner stepped into the clearing when another voice chimed in, "And if they can't handle you, Toughy Badger, I can make you wish you had never been born," warned Ody Skunk.

From above, Big Mouth Bertie Crow called down, "And I will peck your head too, Toughy."

"OK, OK!" Toughy spoke in a sullen voice, "You win — I have never seen a bunch like you!"

"First, Mr. Badger, I would like to explain that we are as you called us, a 'strange bunch,' because we are friends and we care for each other. Secondly," and now Digby began to smile as he spoke, "there is no reason why you can't be part of our strange bunch, if you would like. And just to start things off on the right foot, I have an old house that needs some repairs. You are welcome to it if you think you can fix it up."

"Well-l-l-l-l," the badger began slowly, "I can fix most any kind of place so that I can live in it. What needs fixing?"

Digby grinned, "The back door leaks, I'm afraid."

"No trouble at all. No trouble for, you see, badgers don't worry about building back doors. We don't use back doors because we don't need them!" bragged Toughy. "There's nothing alive in these woods that could keep me from using MY front door — I'll take it!"

"Hooray!" shouted Bouncer as he came bounding across the clearing from his hiding place. "How can I ever thank you folks?" A tear or two came rolling down his furry cheeks.

"No need to," Digby replied shortly, somewhat embarrassed, but everyone in the crowd knew the full meaning of it.

With that, the members of the community gathered around Toughy Badger to welcome him. That is, everyone except Sly Fox who was hiding in his house, and Ody Skunk who remained off to the downwind side out of courtesy toward her friends.

After the greetings were over, they all began moving off toward Digby's house.

As they went, Toughy turned to Digby with a question. "By the way, groundhog, where do you live?"

Digby replied, "Well Mr. Badger, I have started a new house, but just before all the uproar, I ran into a large boulder that I can't move, so I suppose I'll have to start all over."

"Not on your life, groundhog. Lead me to that rock — they don't call me Toughy for nothing."

Fifteen minutes later, amid the cheers of the many onlookers, the big rock, which had brought Digby's digging to a halt, came bumping, jerking, and scraping up the new hallway. With one mighty heave, the badger pushed it out the door and a number of feet down the hillside.

"How can I ever thank you, Mr. Badger?" Digby asked.

"Just don't call me 'Mr.' — that will be thanks enough," laughed Toughy.

"OK, Toughy, and my name is Digby."

"DIGBY ... DIGBY! No sir – none of that – I'll just call you CHUCK!" the rough and tumble badger declared. "CHUCK it is!"

CHAPTER 7

Some Friendly Advice

SPRINGTIME HAD SLIPPED away behind the hot days of summer for many weeks now. As in years gone by, the dry August weather forced Digby and some of his friends to venture out to the clover and alfalfa patches early in the morning. They went both to get breakfast and to drink their fill from the dew on the leaves of the plants. Digby was doing just as his father and grandfathers before him did when the timid little brook no longer had the strength to run. Because of the heat and dry weather it had become just a dry, rocky pathway through the meadow and the woods.

Digby could never quite satisfy his thirst now. It seemed to cause him to become just a little irritable. At times he dreamed to himself, "Oh, for a nice long drink of cool water from the brook like it was in the springtime. I just know that would make me feel wonderful again."

It was one of those hot mid-summer mornings. After Digby had eaten breakfast and sipped his morning dew, he decided to climb to the top of the hill. It was one of his favorite places. Up there he knew the cooler breezes played without bumping into the trees. Up there, even on a hot day one could enjoy life.

On the slow trip to the top of the hill the groundhog met two of his friends, Bouncer Rabbit and Porky Possum. The rabbit was eating breakfast and Porky was doing what he does best, loafing.

"Good morning, gentlemen," came Digby's greeting, "How is this day treating you?"

"Mm-m-m-m-m–ha-m-m-m," gurgled Bouncer. For his mouth was full of clover, you see. "Ah-m-m-m-m, sorry, Chuck, I had to swallow first. Now, oh yes, why things are just fine with me."

Digby winced and frowned at the nickname Toughy Badger had given him. He didn't mind it from the badger, but coming from his best friend it struck a wrong nerve in him. He said nothing, hoping it would not happen again.

"Wall, Dig, ole-boy, it's ah good day fer me too," came the Possum's drawl. "Ma belly's full from last night. Ah do ma eatin' at night, ya know. Ah'm warm from the sun, and this is a nice soft spot whar I'm lyin'. And more than that, y'all are the bestest company fer talkin' to ah could want."

"Glad to hear it," came the reply. "Say, I'm going up to the hilltop for the cooler breezes. Want to come along?"

"Great!" piped the rabbit. "I'm ready to go anytime."

"Sho-nuf," agreed Porky, "but let's walk slo-like. Wha da ya say?"

The trip to the top of the hill was a very lazy one. Each of the of the three friends made their way according to the mood he was in. Bouncer skipped and danced along in a manner that exhibited his carefree way. Porky, on the other hand, shuffled up the pathway with a total unconcerned air about him. Digby moped along, not because he was a mopey individual, but because he had been in a frame of mind lately that was not quite as jaunty as usual. After a time they reached the top of the hill.

The cool, dancing breezes were not long in finding them. They whirled and twirled all about the tired little fellows. It was a most refreshing and classic performance. Digby sat slouched back against a rather large rock with his eyes closed. He should have been totally at peace with the world, but instead, something kept bothering him, something that he could not exactly put his paw on.

Porky was laid out flat on the grass sound asleep, snoring very large possum snores. Nothing was on his mind. Bouncer, as usual, could not be still for long, nor could he be quiet. His chatter was continuous and it came close to being just plain annoying to the grouchy groundhog.

"Hey, Chuck, what are you thinking about?" the mouthy hare inquired as he gave Digby a mild whack on the back. There it was again, that awful nickname that bothered the woodchuck so much. Once more he held his tongue.

"Nothing to speak of," came the sullen reply.

"Oh, come on now, you have to be thinking about something," chided Bouncer.

"Well, if you must know, I've been thinking about that gray ribbon over there that runs off across the hills. It has those different colored bugs creeping along on it. I've thought for a long time that I would like to go there and see it. Now I think I will." Porky slept on soundly as the two talked.

"Chuck, I don't think you ought to go," Bouncer said seriously, "I have heard bad stories about that thing, very bad stories!"

The already irritated groundhog now grew more upset as it seemed that Bouncer was just trying to interfere with his plans, and besides, there was that name again. "What does a dumb rabbit know anyway?" he growled out loud.

Bouncer looked surprised but was not wise enough to drop the subject. "Well! I'll tell you — a couple of my great uncles were killed by those colored bugs, and so was one of yours, smarty!" rattled the gabby rabbit.

"Nevertheless, I'm going to go!" steamed Digby, "so just don't say any more."

"Now, Chuck, why won't you listen ..."

"DON'T CALL ME CHUCK!" roared the totally frustrated Digby. "DON'T CALL ME CHUCK AGAIN!"

Digby had fallen victim to that which traps so many of us. He spoke harshly to someone who had unintentionally been pesty, but did not deserve such harsh treatment. The other side of the story is that Bouncer thoughtlessly continued to pester Digby when he should have recognized that his friend was upset. He should have known that a squabble always requires two squabblers.

The sudden outburst from his friend shocked the mouthy rabbit right back on his powder-puff tail. He took three very large hops away from Digby before he turned to examine the situation. What he saw was the furry, brown back of Digby C. Groundhog as he stalked away down the hillside in the direction of the little-known gray ribbon that twisted and curled its way across the hills.

The worried cries of Bouncer, "Don't go, Digby! Come back! Come back, Digby!" Bouncer called to him with absolutely no effect on the groundhog. All he did was wake Porky Possum from his nap.

"Huh-huh, wha-what's goin' on? Hey, Bouncer, whar's ol Digby a-goin?" he babbled as he rubbed the sleep from his eyes.

"Into trouble, I'm afraid. Into trouble, I'm really afraid," moaned Bouncer, "and I'm afraid I'm to blame, o-o-o-o-o-o." Two rabbit tears trickled down Bouncer's nose and dropped off into the grass.

Digby muttered and grumbled for at least half an hour as he walked. His agitation with Bouncer had taken over his good nature. "Dumb rabbit! Who does he think he is? Calls me 'Chuck!' Oh, how I dislike that name! Then he is always talking and jabbering. How can anyone even think when he is going on? Always trying to tell me what to do. Oh! Don't go, Digby! Ah-h-h, dumb rabbit." On and on went the complaining groundhog, up and down the hills, across small streams and ditches, through brush and across open fields. After a time, though, his grumbling stopped, but his bad mood stayed with him.

For such a hot day, Digby had traveled quite a distance. With the heat of anger inside, he simply didn't notice the heat of the sun outside. He was just coming to a small wooded area after crossing an open field when he spied an old acquaintance jogging along the edge of the woods. The quick trotting gait and shiny red coat made him very easy to recognize. It was Sly Fox. Now under normal circumstances, Digby would have to be very wary of the fox, because when he was hungry he would try to take a meal where he could, but since now he knew that Toughy Badger was Digby's friend, there was little chance he would start trouble.

"Well, hello, Digby!" Sly called out as he drew near. "What in the world are you doing way out here? You are a long way from home."

"Hello, Sly. Yes, I am a long way from home, and if it makes any difference, I'm headed for that gray ribbon that I see from my hilltop," Digby replied rather saltily.

"Oh!" exclaimed Sly, taken back somewhat by the tone in Digby's voice. "I didn't mean to pry. Don't you think, though, that it is kind of dangerous for you to make such a long trip alone?"

"Now look, Sly, don't you start in on me too!" Digby growled fiercely. "Bouncer gave me a big speech about it and I am in no mood to listen to you preach to me also."

"Sorry," said Sly, "I didn't know you were so sensitive to good advice. In spite of that, I'm telling you that it is very dangerous there. Many of my family have been killed by those colored monsters that roar along that 'ribbon,' as you call it."

"Just leave me alone!" cried Digby as he wheeled and plunged off into the woods. "Just leave me alone!" For some reason he could not explain, tears were very close to coming.

He had walked for about half an hour after leaving Sly Fox when he began to hear a buzzing, roaring sound ahead. Every so often he could hear a very musical sound mixed in. Digby wasn't sure if it was the call of a strange animal or not. Suddenly he was aware that the hairs on his back were standing up and quivers of fear shook him from time to time. "Maybe," he said to himself, "I should have listened to them back home and not come here. Oh! Now don't be such a coward, Digby," his curiosity said to him. "How will you ever see this thing for yourself if you don't go on?"

After arguing with himself for a time, Digby went on. His curious nature had won out. He was walking through a wooded area and the sounds were much louder and closer. The woods and brush began to thin out ahead and the sunlight was growing brighter. All of a sudden he was in an opening and there, just over a small, sharp hillside, lay the thing that had brought the groundhog all this way. There was the gray ribbon with the stripe running along its middle.

Digby lay on his stomach and peeked over the edge of the incline, just staring at the ribbon. It looked like nothing he had ever seen before. It did not move as the brook and river did. It had no rocks or roots sticking up out of its surface as did the path on his hillside. It just seemed to be still and dead and without an end.

At that moment from over the hilltop to Digby's right popped a large, red, roaring, boxlike creature which was moving much faster than even Sly Fox could ever run. It stayed on one side of the ribbon, between its edge and the yellow stripe running down its middle. As it rushed by in front of him, the groundhog could smell an odor like nothing he had ever smelled before. It made his eyes burn and his nose felt all filled up with something he disliked very much.

After a fit of coughing and clearing his breathing equipment, Digby peeked over the edge of the hillside just in time to see two more of the strange things. They were smaller in size from the first one. These two things came along on the ribbon from Digby's left side. They were moving along the ribbon on the other side of the yellow stripe from where the first thing had run. Then one of the things moved across the yellow stripe and ran on ahead of the other thing. At that moment, to Digby's surprise, a strange musical cry came from the thing that was moving past the other one. It was the same sound he had heard while he was still out in the woods. It rang out from the throat of the thing as it raced away.

The sound was so loud that Digby clapped his paws over his ears to shut out the cry. His eyes bugged out with fear. Surely it was the cry of some vicious, wild animal. Then in a moment the things were gone out of sight.

After the first shock of the strange sights, sounds, and smells, and having not been harmed by any of them, Digby became less fearful and more curious. He watched for quite a length of time as more of the strange things came zipping by. After a time, he thought to himself, "I think it wouldn't hurt anything if I got a little closer where I could see better." That decision was a very foolish one, as Digby would later realize. It would bring him much trouble and pain.

Down the steep bank he crept. Slowly through the tall grass he made his way. Each time one of the strange creatures whizzed by, he would crouch down out of sight. All over his body rippled quivers of both fear and excitement. Yet after each time one of those things went by, Digby would crawl closer. He couldn't seem to help himself. Shortly, he was in a ditch just by the very edge of the ribbon. He lay still for a time. As luck would have it, none of the strange things came by at that moment. Thinking after a time it was safe to creep closer, he climbed up to the ribbon itself. At last, there he was!

Digby sat just a few inches from it. Then, not knowing just what to do next, he stuck his nose out and sniffed the ribbon. Not finding any smell about it that signaled danger, he touched it.

"Ouuuch!" yelled the startled groundhog. The ribbon was hard and hot! Digby's nose was very tender. Not being satisfied with that, he touched it with his paw. It was still quite warm to the touch but his paws were much tougher than his nose. The heat was not too uncomfortable. Why, he was sure now that he could even walk on the ribbon if he wanted to.

Out in the middle of the ribbon was that stripe he had always wondered about from his hilltop. Now, since he had come this far, why not examine it up close? Not being able to find a reason not to go closer, Digby stepped out on the ribbon and cautiously crept to the stripe.

It was a very bright thing when he got up close. As of yet he had not figured out what it was. It did not move. It lay very flat on the ribbon. What indeed was it? As he sat there gazing at the yellow stripe, the woodchuck forgot all about the possibility of danger. Too late, he became aware of the fast-approaching sound of one of those strange things that use the ribbon as their pathway. Back toward the ditch Digby whirled, but he was not quick enough.

In his ears was a madness of sound. The whining of the thing, its musical cry, and then a high-pitched scream much like that of the hawks that circle his meadow from time to time. All of it crashed upon his mind.

Digby had almost reached the edge of the ribbon and the safety of the ditch which lay just ahead of him when a terrible blinding explosion of pain struck him from behind. For a moment he saw everything as though it were upside down. Then came a huge cluster of bright lights before his eyes. Then his mind became wrapped in a blanket of pure blackness.

Digby began dreaming of his hilltop and the timid brook that ran lazily through the meadow. He saw the sweet grasses waving in the breeze. All the wonderful places he called home went swimming through his clouded mind. Other images came and went before him but he just couldn't quite make them out.

In his pain and dreams, figures and faces flitted in and out of his sight. He just couldn't quite make them out. It seemed to Digby that someone kept calling his name but he simply could not answer. Finally he managed to open one eye, just barely. His eyelids were terribly heavy but he could for a moment make out the image of a fuzzy little face set with two big round eyes. It looked like great big tears were streaming down from them in a flood.

Then, regaining a bit of his senses, the groundhog realized that never in his whole life had he been so glad to see Bouncer Rabbit, even if he was crying. Then, with a sigh, Digby slipped back into a deep sleep.

When Digby had disappeared down the hill in a fit of anger, Porky Possum was not yet fully awake from his afternoon nap. But then Bouncer's wails and moans got his attention and began to make sense to him. "You mean that ole Digby has sur-nuff gone off by hisself to see Two Legs' road?" he asked.

"Yes-yes!" cried the rabbit. "Yes, he has, and I just know that something dreadful will happen to him. Porky, what can we do?"

"Wall – I don't rightly know. Seems to me that ole Digby was kinda put out with you. I'm not sure he'll let us do anything," came the reply.

"I know – I know, and it's all my fault." Bouncer was now wringing his paws and pacing back and forth. "But we have to do something anyway. I know—let's gather the folks of the meadow together. With all of us thinking we can certainly find an answer. Come on Porky – hurry!"

The trip back down the hillside was much faster than the one coming up earlier. In a short time a community council had been called under Chatty Squirrel's tree.

"Quiet! QUIET!" Bertie Crow squalled from a limb on the tree. "Now let Bouncer talk!"

"Thank you, Bertie. My friends, we must do something quickly. Digby has been a special friend to all of us at one time or another, and a real friend to us all of the time. Now he is walking into a danger that he doesn't understand. What can we do to help him?" Bouncer cast his eyes from one side of the group to the other.

"We could just go and haul him back," Toughy Badger called out.

"No, no," said Chatty Squirrel, "that would just make him more upset than he already is."

"How about running on ahead of him, hiding in the bushes, and scaring him into returning home?" suggested Speedy Turtle.

"Ho-ho-ho," laughed Sneaky Weasel, "and just how do you expect to get ahead of him at the rate you move, Speedy?"

"Not me, you ignorant weasel, but someone who can cover the distance very fast," answered the exasperated turtle. "You ignorant weasel!"

All of the group laughed at the embarrassed turtle. Then Wiseman Owl spoke. "Wouldn't it be easier just to watch over him, but at the same time let him do his exploring? I think Bertie here could do the job very well. If trouble comes, he can let us know and we can find a way then to help."

"Good idea!" shouted many in the group as they all recognized that would be the way they would want things done if they were in Digby's place.

"OK then, Bertie," shouted an excited Bouncer, "on your way. Digby may be there by now! Come on – hurry!"

"OK–OK," squawked the crow as he lifted off from his perch. "I'm going–I'm going!"

With that a cheer went up from the crowd on the ground. Bertie circled once and then flew off toward the gray ribbon in the distance across the hills.

It took some time and a bit of flying before Bertie spotted the small brown object below. One look was all he needed to realize that a lot of help was soon to be needed for his friend down there sitting in the middle of the gray ribbon. He seemed to be staring at the yellow streak that ran along the middle of the ribbon. Then, off around the nearby bend in the ribbon, Bertie could see one of those strange, shiny things approaching very fast. His call of warning was of no use. He was too high and the wind would just carry his call away.

At the last moment, the crow could see Digby wheel and scoot away for the weeds at the edge of the ribbon. Too late he had tried to escape. The shiny thing struck Digby a glancing blow. Bertie could see him go flying through the air to land in the weeds just in front of him. Bertie squeezed his eyes shut for a moment, feeling Digby's pain. Then he dived almost straight down to land at his friend's side.

It took only a moment for Bertie to find that by himself he could do nothing to help Digby. Up into the sky he leaped and, clearing the nearby treetops, he sped off toward the meadow and help.

Practically everyone in the meadow wanted to make the trip to try and help Digby. The news which Bertie brought spread quickly. In a short period of time a very worried crowd was gathered at Chatty's tree. After many wild suggestions of how to help their injured friend, once again it was the wise advice of Professor Owl that they followed.

"I know everyone here wants to go," he said, "but that will cause too much confusion. We could only travel as fast as the slowest in the group. On the other hand, some of us can get there quite fast by flying, but we don't have the strength to move Digby. I suggest that Bertie lead the way and that two or three of the strongest among us who can travel reasonably fast make the trip. Maybe they can find a way to get him home."

"Yes – yes!" they all cried. "But who should go?"

"I'll go," called out Toughy Badger. "I'll carry him home on my back if others will help by seeing that he doesn't fall off."

"I'll do that," shouted out Ringo Coon.

"Me too," added Porky Possum.

"I must go too!" cried Bouncer. "Digby is my best friend – and he might not be in this situation if I had been kinder to him and not called him by a name he disliked. I MUST GO!" The anxious rabbit paced back and forth, shaking his head and looking fearfully off in the direction where Digby lay injured.

Chatty piped up, "All right, if everyone is agreed, you

four start on your way immediately!" With many wishes of good luck and hopes that Digby might be found not too seriously injured, the party set off through the woods.

The rescue party made excellent time getting to the place where the injured groundhog lay among the weeds. The last few yards down the slope to where Digby lay were covered at a gallop. Bouncer was the first of the group on the ground to arrive at his friend's side. Bertie was already there waiting on the others.

The rabbit bent over his friend and cried out his name over and over. "DIGBY! Oh! Digby! Please wake up – Oh! Digby, won't you please wake up? Speak to me – please open your eyes and speak to me. PLEASE!"

At first there was no response. Then there was a very slight fluttering of Digby's eyelids. After further pleading by the almost hysterical rabbit, both eyes opened a slight bit and Bouncer felt certain his friend knew him. Then came a weak whisper.

"You aa-are m-my friend. I-I should h-have listened to you."

Then Digby dropped off into a deep sleep and the journey home began.

CHAPTER 8

A Ring Around Ringo

THE TRIP BACK to the meadow was slow and painful. After much pushing with snouts, and puffing and grunting, the limp body of the groundhog had been slid upon the broad back of Toughy Badger. With Ringo Coon on one side and Porky Possum on the other, both walked close against the side of Toughy. The totally dedicated group of Digby's friends struggled to balance Digby's body on its delicate perch.

Bouncer scurried from side to side, giving all kinds of excited instructions but not really doing much to help— except that he was constantly trying to comfort poor Digby. They had traveled part of the way home when the injured groundhog began to regain his senses. "Oh-o-o-o-o," he groaned. "Oh! My head – oh, my back. Wha - what happened?"

"Digby! Digby, thank goodness you're awake! You were hit by one of those things back there on the gray ribbon," chattered Bouncer in an almost delirious voice. "We were afraid you had been killed – but you're alive!"

"Just take it easy, Digby. We will be as careful as we can, and we will soon have you back home," advised Ringo.

"Yo-all are one lucky woodchuck, Dig, ole boy," drawled Porky. "Yah could-a saved yoreself a lot-a trouble if you'd-a listened to some friendly advice, yah know."

"I know now you are right, Porky," Digby agreed with a little shake of his head.

"Seems like we-all have to learn some things by feelin' the pain instead of listenin' to good advice," observed the slow-talking Possum.

Through the conversation Bouncer had been very silent, at least for him. He had been walking with his head drooping down and his eyes were cast on the ground at his feet. Now he moved closer to Digby and began in a very serious tone. "Digby, I'm so sorry! I will never call you 'Chuck' again. And I will never try to tell you what to do, or what not to do. Please forgive me. All of this was my fault, and I am SO SORRY!" Large rabbit tears flowed down his furry cheeks in a steady stream.

"Toughy," said Digby, "please stop and put me down for a rest."

"OK, Chuck, I need a little breather myself." With the help of his rescuers, Digby was soon sitting leaned up against the trunk of a large oak tree and resting.

"Now, Bouncer," he began in a voice that was growing stronger, "you dry those tears and listen to me. I got hurt because of my own foolishness, and not because of what other folks did or said. I was grouchy to begin with. One thing led to another, and I did not have the good sense to control my feelings. I wouldn't listen to sound advice. And most of all, I was very foolish when danger was near. I let my curiosity overpower my good sense. No, my friend, you did not cause me to get hurt—not at all. I did that myself."

"Thank you! Thank you for that, Digby," replied the sniffling rabbit. "But I could never have lived with myself if you had been killed."

At that moment Bertie Crow came swirling down out of the sky to land beside the resting groundhog. "O-ho! So you decided to stop being such a lazy sleepyhead, I see. This business of taking long naps in the middle of the day will have to stop, Mr. Groundhog," chided the talky crow. "Just where are you hurt?"

"My back and my hind legs mostly, and I have a big bump on my head," came the quavery reply.

"That is where you landed. Right on your hard woodchuck head," cackled Bertie. "A few days rest and you

93

will be as good as new – you'll see."

"How do you know I landed on my head?" inquired the puzzled Digby.

"I saw you get hit by that thing. The sight of it almost made me go into a spin and crash from the fear of it!" Bertie replied.

"And how did you happen to be up there over top of me at the time, may I ask?" Digby questioned.

"Wel-l-l-l, uh,–we–er, well we all were afraid that you would run into trouble in the frame of mind you were in when you left us. So-o-o, we–er–we all decided that I would kind of–kind of watch over you from a distance," stammered the embarrassed crow.

"And just who is 'we', may I ask?" Digby was a bit indignant, but not for long.

"Well–uh, it was everyone in the meadow. We had a community meeting, and after much discussion, Professor Owl suggested the plan. Uh–because we all love you, Digby." Bertie was very serious now.

"Do you mean all the woodsfolk were concerned about me?" Digby's voice was quavering now with emotion.

"Everyone!" stated Toughy with firmness. "Everyone!"

Digby sat silent for a time and then said quietly, "I never knew I had so many friends. Until now I never really understood how important friends are."

Bouncer piped up, "Being a friend to others, like you are to us, is the very best way to gain friends. And friends are very important! I believe that what, or who, ever made us and put us here in this meadow is very sad when we are not being friends, but is very happy when we are friends with each other."

Digby looked at Bouncer and after a moment spoke, "Bouncer, you surprise me. I never knew that you thought that deeply about things. But you know, I think you are absolutely right about that!"

The hot summer nights had now passed. The leaves and the grasses were beginning to show their age. They were displaying a slight tint of yellowish-brown in their colors where not long ago there was a brilliant green. The fall season of the year had come upon the land and summer was just a memory.

Digby had recovered quite well from his injuries with the exception of a small amount of stiffness in his joints just before stormy weather was about to set in. He had been very well cared for by his meadow community friends.

One evening Ringo Coon and Porky Possum came to sit with Digby on his front porch. Of course Bouncer was there, as he was many times each day. They enjoyed the beautiful fall sunsets that happened almost every evening now that there were few leaves to blot out the sunlight.

"Shore seems like every new sunset is purtier than the last one, don't it?" observed Porky.

"Too bad so many folks in this world never take time to look at a sunset, or the moon shining on fluffy clouds. I really believe that whatever made us is also the best at making other beautiful things. We just need to take the time to notice them," Ringo said with a touch of gentleness in his voice.

Digby agreed, "That's true, Ringo. I suppose you know

more about the beautiful things of the nighttime since you do much of your traveling after dark."

"Wall, I don't know about that, Digby," reminded Porky, "Yah know I get around a lot at night too."

"And so do I, at times," chimed in Bouncer.

"Hm-m-m-m, seems like I'm the one who doesn't get around much after the sun goes down," Digby admitted.

"Yo-all don't know what fun yore missin', Dig, ole buddy," Porky commented, "Yo ought-a come out some night with us and enjoy yo-self."

"Just what kind of fun would we have?" the groundhog inquired.

"Well now," began Ringo, "Two Legs has started chasing me at night again with his dog. Maybe we could figure out a way to have some fun with the mutt. He is really not very smart, you know."

"Hey! That sounds like a good time!" The rabbit was dancing with glee. "Lets see now, what can we do to that old hound that we haven't done before? We have run him in circles for years now. I can't think of anything new at the moment."

"Maybe that's the answer. Why not do the same old thing, only more of it this time?" questioned Digby.

"What yo-all got on your mind, Dig?" puzzled Porky.

"Listen, if we were to give that old hound more trails to follow than he could handle, it might make for an interesting evening," came the answer.

Ringo's eyes brightened, "I get it. We will get 'Mutt' to start chasing me and then the rest of you can get into the act. Right?"

"What act?" inquired Bertie Crow as he taxied up from a perfect landing. "What's going on?"

The idea was explained to the crow, who let out a grand squawk of pleasure. In a moment he took off into the air shouting back over his wings as he went, "I'll go tell the rest of the folks. They'll all want in on the fun."

"They sure don't call him BIG MOUTH BERTIE for nothing," observed Ringo.

"Since it seems that everyone in the meadow is going to be in on this event, we had better go over our plan to make certain everything is clear," Digby advised. Everyone in the group agreed and shortly they were busy with preparations for the evening.

Two Legs and his dog had pestered the meadow community for years. Ringo, Bouncer, Chatty, Sly, Zippy Quail, Cocky Pheasant, and many others had been the object of Two Legs' hunting trips. They all looked forward now to turning the tables on the one who had made life dangerous for them. Especially they wanted to give Mutt, the dog, a taste of his own medicine. Tonight they would.

The moon did not show its face that night. A slight breeze rustled among the leaves and grasses. It was just enough of a breeze to cover the sounds of stealthy movements in the dark. It was a perfect setting for what the woodsfolk had planned.

About two hours after the sun had crouched behind the hills, the signal came floating down from the sky. "Hooo-ooo—get ready! They are coming," Professor Owl called down as he circled in the darkness.

With that, Ringo set off in a circling course which

took him across the pathway over which the hunters would soon come. The scent of the coon would tickle the nose of Mutt and he would tell the world all about his discovery. "Awoooooo- Awoo- Awoooo-oo," he would bellow out to the night sky. In a few moments that is exactly what he did.

Ringo set his course according to plan. Down the hill to the timid brook, across the string-of-pearls rock bridge, down the far side of the creek bank to a fallen tree which stretched across the stream, and then back up the other side of the stream to Chatty's tree scurried the grinning ringtail.

Upon reaching the tree he made three circles around the trunk of the tree, with each one of them growing farther and farther away from the tree. The third time around the tree brought Ringo to the edge of the creek, where he simply slipped into the water and swam away.

Mutt's bellows could be heard as he tracked the trail of the coon. The pearl bridge and the fallen tree had slowed him down so that by the time he reached Chatty's tree, Ringo was hidden on the far creek bank where he could see the fun.

Upon reaching the tree, the dog began to follow the track in circles, trying to unscramble the confusing trail. After a time of worried sniffing and baying, the panting dog sat down under the tree for a short rest, saying to himself in an agitated growl, "Now where did that smart-aleck coon duck off to this time?"

It was at that point when Chatty got into the action. Taking very careful aim, she pushed a recently gathered hickory nut out of her front door. She watched it fall into the gloom toward the shadowy figure below. Her aim was deadly. The nut landed with a loud, hollow "POP!"–squarely on the top of the hound dog's head.

"Owoooo-oo," yowled the surprised dog.

Now that small nut did no real damage to Mutt. It just caused him to express his surprise. He looked up, trying to locate the source of that pesky nut. That was when he got the real surprise. Close behind the little hickory nut that Chatty had launched came a much larger walnut. Her aim once again was accurate. The walnut, which still wore its heavy summer husk, smacked squarely into Mutt's upturned nose with a loud and resounding, "SPLATT!"

The startled dog let go with a very loud yowl, much louder than the first one, "AWOOOO-OOOO!! OH! MY NOSE! My nose is surely broken! It's bent. Oh! Oh! My nose–OO-OOO!" In a rush, the dog made for the creek and plunged his snout into the cool water to ease the hurt. It was at that moment that Ringo set out once more to lay another trail that would lead old Mutt into even greater trouble.

Meanwhile, from the bushes along the creek came snickers and giggles and muffled laughter. The woodsfolk were having a real good time that night at the expense of a nasty dog who had not treated them very nicely for a long time.

Up on a hilltop away from the meadow, Two Legs stopped to listen to the baying and bellowing of his coon-hunting dog. "That is a beautiful sound," he thought to himself. When Mutt let out his yowl of surprise from the falling walnut, Two Legs was a little concerned, but hearing nothing further he paid no more attention. Little did he know at the time that before the night was over, he too would be letting out a few howls of surprise.

Ringo loped along the brookside once more to the fallen tree over which he again crossed the stream. Zigzagging through the bushes and around the hillside, he passed quietly within a few yards of where Two Legs stood listening for Mutt's bellow.

After soothing his aching nose, Mutt made his way up the creek bank close to where Ringo had been hiding. Soon the dog's sensitive nose picked up the scent of the coon and the chase was on once more.

After passing the man, Ringo slowed down so that Mutt could get closer. When the yowling of the dog had grown near enough, the coon headed straight for Sly Fox's home on the little hill by the brook. Sly was waiting there as planned. As Ringo drew near, Sly joined in the chase close beside him. Side by side the two friends trotted away.

For a time the two ran side-by-side, very close together. Then, upon reaching a large rock close to the front door of Digby's new home, they parted and took paths that led in opposite directions.

Mutt had suddenly become confused. The scent of the trail had changed. One moment he was sure he was chasing the coon. But the next moment the trail smelled like a fox. Unable to figure out the mystery, he finally decided just to chase whatever up ahead was making the trail.

The dog charged up to the large rock, bellowing loudly as he ran. "Awooooo- awooooo, all right whatever you are,

I've got you now," he squalled. Suddenly the big rock loomed in the darkness in front of him. Only an emergency sliding stop saved him from crashing headlong into that large stone. At this point Mutt became even more confused.

Now it seemed that the unknown animal he was chasing had broken in half, with one part going one direction smelling like a coon, while the other part went the other direction smelling like a fox. Mutt stopped, sat down, scratched a flea, and muttered to himself, "Now what's going on here? This chase is nothing like it normally is!"

Unknowingly, Mutt had taken a seat not far from Digby's front door, which was just behind him. More than that, both Digby and Toughy Badger waited just inside for the right moment. Mutt had finished scratching and decided to rest for a moment when the darkness behind him erupted in a storm of ferocious growls, snarls, groundhog whistles, and badger threats. None of those terrible noises made any sense to him, even though during all of the growls and hisses both Digby and Toughy were shouting all kinds of catcalls and jibes at him.

Mutt was so frightened he did not know which way to run. In fact, he did not run. He managed two terrified leaps in the darkness away from the sound before he stumbled over the large rock and tumbled into a large prickly thorn bush close by. The hound's yelps and howls of discomfort could be heard for quite a distance. He managed to scramble out of the thorn bush and galloped away, looking for Two Legs and some sympathy.

Once again the whole community was filled with

laughter. They were the ones who had been chased and frightened by that dog and Two Legs for so many years.

After being consoled and babied a little by the man, the dog and his master made their way down the hillside by the light of the lantern which Two Legs carried. The woodsfolk knew exactly where they were at all times because of that light.

Ringo went on ahead and laid down a new trail in front of the two hunters in a way that Mutt could hardly miss it. Soon the musical bellows of the hunting hound danced in and out among the trees. The chase had begun anew.

Down the near side of the timid brook they went in a zig-zag, in and out, around and around pattern. Mutt was happy once more because he was doing what he was born for and what he liked best. He was chasing his quarry as he had been trained to do. So intent was he with the hunt that he did not realize that now he had become the one who was being hunted.

As Ringo sped along, Mutt followed in hot pursuit, but just behind him a shadowy figure loped along easily. Sly Fox was trailing Mutt. Shortly Sly was joined by Porky and Ody Skunk. Toughy Badger soon appeared along with Doty Deer. In the dark night sky above two silent winged objects also followed the baying dog. Bertie and the Professor were flying side-by-side above the unfolding scene below. As fast as they could catch up, Chatty Squirrel, Sneaky Weasel, and Digby joined the nighttime parade. The time had come for a great ending to this wildwood drama.

Two Legs was drinking in the sweet music of his baying dog's voice. It was not difficult for him to follow the course of the chase. Mutt's bellows followed down the creek for a while, then turned up the far side of the hill. It circled and zig-zagged in some heavy brush, then headed toward the hilltop. The man was sure the trail was leading back in his direction—and so it was.

As the sound of the chase moved over the top of the hill a change came over its sound. At first Two Legs thought that Mutt's voice was giving out. He would bark as usual but then would come a high-pitched howl or maybe a shrill squeal, followed by a growl that certainly did not sound like Mutt.

"What in blazes is the matter with that crazy dog?" said Two Legs out loud. At that instant he could hear a thrashing sound in the tall weeds on the hillside just above where he was standing. Ringo Coon suddenly burst out of the darkness into the circle of light made by the man's lantern. The coon charged right past the startled man. Two Legs turned to watch the fleeing coon and was immediately struck a heavy blow on top of his head by a large feathered object that swooped down out of the sky. The lantern went flying as the man stumbled backward. Professor Owl was right on target. Bertie Crow, though not much of a night flyer, came diving in right behind the Professor. Flitter Sparrow, who had joined the battle, along with Zippy Quail, also added the weight of their small bird bodies to the attack. That was enough to put Two Legs flat on his back, covering his head and floundering in the darkness, which was only lighted a bit by the flickering lantern sitting in the grass.

Just then Mutt came galloping through the scene in

hot pursuit of Ringo. Too late he saw his fallen master on whose face he unfortunately stepped as he went by.

The man tried to sit up and regain his sense of direction but now came a great rush of whistling, growling, squealing, snapping figures who each in turn bounced and jostled the terrified man most disrespectfully. The rush was over in a moment.

Two Legs by that time was in a state of panic. He did not even wait to pick up his lantern or his hat which had fallen off in the riot. Up the hill and across the fields in the direction of his house he ran, with fear stepping on his heels all the way home. To be certain, it would be a long time before Two Legs would hunt the woodsfolk again.

As for Mutt, the chase was not over yet.

CHAPTER 9

Anything Can Change

MUTT DID NOT realize that now it was he who was the object of the chase, not Ringo. The coon continued to play his part very well. On through the darkness the strange parade continued.

After Two Legs left the scene in total fright, the

woodsfolk turned their attention to Mutt. Bellowing, barking, and baying is what a good hunting dog does best while on a trail. At that, though, he must rest his voice now and then. It was during one of those brief rest periods when Mutt became aware that all was not as it should be. Just as the echoes of his own voice died away, from behind him came a shrill, "Yap, Yap," accompanied by other growls and squeals of many kinds. The hair on Mutt's back stood straight up and it was not from anger.

The dog's first instinct was to turn and fight in self defense. But as soon as he moved in that direction he became aware that many bodies were crashing through the weeds and brush toward him. Mutt's next thought was to run for home. As he turned in that direction, his way was blocked by the large body of Doty Deer and by the hisses and snarls of Ringo Coon, who had now turned to confront his tormentor. The only way left for the cornered dog was down along the bank of the timid brook. Away he ran with the howling, screeching, squalling, and now sometimes laughing crowd of victorious woodsfolk in hot pursuit.

"Catch him!"

"Run him into a hole in the ground!"

"Put him up a tree just like he did to us!"

"Bite his tail and pull the hair out of it! That's what he does!"

And so the catcalls went. But no one really intended to seriously hurt Mutt. They just wanted to teach him a lesson he would not soon forget.

Mutt ran as fast as he could, but he was to learn that some of the woodsfolk could run faster than he. Sly Fox and Doty Deer had no trouble staying right on the heels of the terrified dog. But it was Professor Owl who would put the finishing touches to the race.

The trail ran for a long distance just beside the creek. At times it ran almost at the water's edge. At other times it ran along the tops of small hillocks, some of which had slid away into the creek during severe storms. It was at the top of one of those miniature landslides that Professor Owl decided to attack the dog from above.

The sharp drop-off where the attack came actually cut back a bit under the hilltop, forming a dangerous spot in the trail. In a quick, swooping dive topped with a shout of "RUN, MUTT! RUN–I'M GOING TO GET YOU, MUTT! RUN!" The Professor plopped right down on the dog's back long enough to deliver a sharp dig with his mighty talons.

Mutt let loose with a mighty, "YAHHH-oooooooooo– Get off! –GET OFF!" Turning his head to try and knock that thing off his back, the dog ran off the trail and along the very edge of the overhang of the cliff. In a split second the ground gave way, taking with it the howling, yowling dog in a shower of falling dirt and small stones. Then everything was quiet.

Shortly, the slower runners came puffing up to stare over the edge of the landslide with the others. After a few moments a low, pitiful moan came from the darkness below. That was followed by a whimpered, "Help me, please, someone help me."

After a time of complete quiet, Digby spoke up, "I think we have done enough. It sounds to me like we need to get down there and try to help Mutt. We can't leave him hurt even after all the things he has done to us. Let's go!"

"Not me!" exclaimed Sly Fox. "That dog has pestered me for years now and I think the score is even. Besides, if we go down there and nothing is seriously wrong with him, Mutt will have one of us for supper."

"Did Mutt ever do more than just chase you, Sly?" Doty's voice was quiet and gentle.

"No—not really, I guess," replied the shamed fox.

"He never hurt me either, but then he never caught me either. I don't know what he would have done if he had got me," Bouncer said with some apprehension.

"But you can only suppose those things, Bouncer, since Mutt never did catch you," came the reply.

"His cousin tore some of my tail feathers out once," squawked Bertie.

Now the Professor replied in his teacher-like manner, "Just remember, Mutt did just what Two Legs taught him to do. And whether we like it or not, Mutt is actually one of us. He and Sly here are distant relatives, you know."

"Is that true, Sly?" asked Ody, sucking in her breath with amazement. She was standing downwind at the far edge of the group as a matter of politeness. "Are you really related to Mutt?"

"Wel-l-l, yes, if you must know, I am. But it is way back on my family tree, you know," came the embarrassed reply.

"Look! I have an idea," Digby said with authority. "Come on—all of you—come with me. I'm going down where Mutt is to try and help him. He needs help!"

The group hesitated, then began to slowly follow Digby down the hillside. They knew that most of the time he had a good sense of what to do. "Here! Let me go first," directed Toughy Badger. "If there is any fight left in that hound, it is best that he meet me first."

Slowly and cautiously the group made their way to the bottom of the cliff at the edge of the creek. There they came upon a mound of dirt and rocks. At first Mutt could not be located. Then the sharp night-trained eyes of Professor Owl spotted the upper half of the dog's head sticking out of the mound of dirt.

A weak voice came from the dirt pile, "Oh! Please, someone help me—oh"—came the weak voice of the defeated dog.

"Hurry! All of you diggers—get in here with me and get busy!" came the sharp command from Digby.

Without another word, Toughy Badger, Bouncer, Ringo, Chatty, Porky, Sly, and Sneaky Weasel all jumped into the work with Digby. The others helped the best they could, but most of those folks, the deer, crow, owl, and quail were not well equipped to move dirt. Ody could have helped as she was a good digger, but if she had stepped into the work area, all the others would not have been able to work due to the natural aroma she carried with her wherever she went. So from a distance she gracefully encouraged the other workers and stood guard in case Two Legs might return.

With so many strong and practiced digging paws at the work, it was but a short time until the dog was uncovered. The large rocks and pieces of a dead log which had fallen down on Mutt were easily handled by Toughy Badger. At last the dog was free from his imprisonment.

As the fact dawned on the woodsfolk that the nasty old dog was no longer held fast by the pile of dirt, they suddenly stepped back to a safer distance. Each one was ready at a moment's notice to dash away for safety. One hint of threat from Mutt and off they would go. In fact, though, they had no reason to fear. Mutt lay still, only whimpering now and then. He was badly bruised and was still quite dizzy. For the moment he was not a threat to anyone.

Digby finally edged slowly to the dog, who was still lying where he had fallen. "Mutt!–Mutt! Can you hear me, Mutt? Can you speak to me? I am Digby Groundhog. Can you speak?"

"Ye-s," came a weak whisper. "Wh-o did you say you are?"

"It's me–Digby Groundhog."

"Dig-by, why are you here?"

"Mutt, there are many others of the meadow community also here with me. We were all chasing you before you fell. When we realized you were hurt, which was partly our fault, we decided to try to help you," explained the groundhog.

"Tha-ank you, thank you. I know–I know you–didn't have to–do that, Why are–you helping me? I–I haven't treated–you folks very–well over the years. That's–that's all over–now. After helping–me like this–I could never be–nasty to you–again. No–never." With that Mutt closed his eyes. He was in a deep sleep, which was the best thing for him just now.

The next morning, long after the sun had scrambled above the treetops and was warming everything, Mutt's eyes slowly opened. The dog finally roused up from the faraway sleep world of the night before. Now he became aware of an even stranger scene before him.

He had been dragged to the edge of the timid brook. His face had been bathed a number of times with clumps of grass wetted in the cool water of the stream. Wild food of many kinds had been laid close by his head during the night. Sitting close by in a circle around him were all the little woodsfolk who for many years had been the object of his hunting trips, along with Two Legs, his master.

It took a few minutes for Mutt's head to clear, and he could begin to remember what had happened the night before. It was becoming clear to him that the very woodsfolk he had chased all those years were the very ones who had rescued him from the dirt pile and cared for him through the night. Now he felt terribly ashamed, but thankful at the same time.

Finally he spoke, "I—I don't know what to say. By the way that many people think, you should never have helped me after the way I have treated you all these years. You are different. You all seem to be so friendly. Why?"

Digby spoke up. "Mutt, you need to understand that being treated badly is no good reason to do the same to those who try to hurt you. We think that whatever made us and put us here is good, and wants us to treat each other in a good way too. We only wanted to tease you, not see you get hurt. Now we hope you can be friendly toward us." He took a breath and continued.

"You are an animal just as we are. You live on Two Legs' farm while we live here in the meadow. But we all were put here by the same One who made everything. We need to share this world. Don't you see that we all are happier when things are peaceful and happy. That is much better than always trying to hurt each other."

"Digby," Professor Owl spoke up, "I could not have said that better, or more beautifully."

"I second the motion," Doty added. "You have learned much this summer about friendship, you have to admit, Digby."

"Thank you both. Coming from you I have to believe that and take it as a compliment," replied the groundhog. "Well, Mutt, what is your answer? What do you have to say?"

The injured hound was silent for a short while. Then he looked around the circle of waiting faces. Finally he answered, "The only answer I believe I can possibly give is, YES! I want to be your friend. I will never chase you again! If my master makes me go hunting, I will lead him away from you. All he wants is to hear the sound of my voice when I'm on a trail and I can bellow and bay anywhere in the dark. The only thing that bothers me is that I don't know how I will ever be able to repay you for being so kind to me when I got hurt." With that, Mutt hung his head and stared at the ground.

Doty Deer's voice came loud and clear now in a firm answer. "Mutt, a real friend expects no pay for an act of friendship. As well, a real friend is always ready to help when there is help needed. As you grow in friendship, I'm certain you will get your chance to be a friend and help someone."

CHAPTER 10

Friendship in the Snow

AFTER RESTING ALL that day, followed by a good night's rest, and relaxing for the second day, Mutt finally started on his journey home. He started off toward Two Legs' farm, very slowly at first as he was still quite stiff and sore, but as he traveled his body began to feel better.

Before he left the meadow community, he made a short speech to all the woodsfolk gathered there.

Mutt began slowly because he was so touched by the kindness that he had never expected. A kindness given with no hesitation on the part of the folks who lived in Friendship Meadow. "I don't know how to thank you folks. I probably won't ever be able to do so completely. You treated me far better than I would have done for you. I just didn't know about friendship and caring for others." He hesitated for a moment, caught his breath and wiped what was an almost-tear from his eye, then went on.

"I was always taught to do my best to catch you if I was on your trail. And if I did, I was expected to do the worst things to you. But, you know, I don't know why Two Legs wanted me to act that way. He's that way about everything. He has never treated me very good either. I've been whipped by him for things I never understood." Again the dog hesitated as he collected his thoughts, then continued.

"I want you folks to know that from this day on, I will never chase any of you again. When Two Legs makes me go hunting, I may run down through the meadow, and I will say hello as I go by, but I will not treat any of you badly ever again. You will hear me bellowing, baying, and barking, but that will only be for the man's ears. Maybe I can even stop by and visit with you when he isn't looking. Now I must go back, but I want you all to know how much I think of you. Please keep on caring for each other as you do and this will be one of the happiest places around. Good-by now—good-by!" And off Mutt went, hobbling his way home.

Most of the trees had lost their summer leaves by now. The nights were getting quite chilly and the sun moved through the sky much closed to the southern skyline than it did during the summer. It seemed like the daylight hours were fewer in number and the nighttime lasted longer and longer. Still, the folks of the meadow were out and about each day, though the kind of things they were doing were different now from those during the summer.

The group of closest friends still gathered most evenings, when it wasn't raining, up on the hillside close to Digby's front door to watch the amazing sunsets of the late fall. Often they would talk about serious things, though every now and then they would have a good laugh over the way Two Legs ran wildly away after the woodsfolk had played the tricks on him in the dark.

On clear nights many times the community would hear the musical voice of Mutt as he ran through the fields and woods pretending to hotly track some imaginary animal so that Two Legs could get his enjoyment while never being a threat to any of the woodsfolk. Once in a while he would run the imaginary trail down through the meadow. As he ran along he would call out, "Hollooooo, my good friends! Ho-o-o-pe you all are well and happy. Isn't it a beau--u-u-u-tiful night. You take care now-w-w-w. See you later!"

The feelings of love, though seldom spoken, were a very strong force in Friendship Meadow. The folks there cared for each other. They were interested in the interests of the others. They helped when needed without being asked. It was a good life.

One evening the sky was painted with beautiful red,

gold, and purple splotches and streaks of color from the setting sun. As the brilliant splash of crimson gushed down from the sky and settled all around the group, Bouncer exclaimed, "I think this one is more beautiful than all the others we have seen!"

"Oh! You say that every time we watch the sun set," scoffed Toughy Badger.

"That's the way it should be." Doty Deer's voice was soft and clear as she walked up to the group.

"I can tell you this. The things we see and feel should be strong, including our memories." Digby got very serious for a time as he talked. He did that more often now since his narrow escape from death over the hills on the gray ribbon.

"You know, I have come to believe that whatever put us here also has something to do with all those beautiful colors up there in the sky. I can't explain it, but I just feel that way. As soon as the sun goes down we say, 'That was the most beautiful sunset I've ever seen,' but it soon becomes a memory. Then when we are watching the next sunset, we say, 'Now isn't that just the most beautiful sunset you have ever seen?' Memories of sunsets are good but the best sunset is the one we are watching at the moment. The Maker of sunsets somehow makes each one better than the last one!"

"Well said, Digby," Doty Deer remarked. "A sunset can never be captured as it really is because it is always changing. So just enjoy each one at the moment you are looking at it and thank the Sunset Painter for allowing us to see such beautiful things."

"Well, I like the moonrise just about as much," said Sly Fox. "That is a pretty sight too. They probably come from the same One who makes the sunrises and sunsets."

"Yes! Oh! My yes!," chirped up Bouncer. "Especially like the one we will have tonight. Oh, how I love to go out and play in the moonlight. In fact, that is exactly what I plan to do tonight."

Digby yawned, "I'm going to go to bed early tonight. It seems as though lately I can sleep and sleep, and still get up sleepy."

"Please, Digby!" the excited rabbit chattered, "Please stay up long enough to see the moon rise–please!"

The drowsy reply came, "Well-ll, OK. But not longer than that. Br-r-r-r, it's getting chilly. And have you noticed? The wind is beginning to blow from the east. It doesn't come from that direction very often. It's kind of unusual. The air feels so damp."

"Winter is very close by, my friends," observed Doty, "very close."

The little group sat and talked for another hour. Almost without notice, the moon slipped up into the sky. In fact, they almost missed the moonrise because of their conversation. "Look at that moon!" Bouncer was overflowing with joy at the sight of it. "Isn't it beautiful tonight?"

"It is, but look at that great big hazy ring around it. That usually means some trouble from the weather," Toughy commented. "Better not play out-of-doors too long tonight, Bouncer."

"Well, now, Mr. Badger! It is too nice of an evening to be spoiled by bad weather!" Bouncer spoke with determination. "Anyway, I have been out in it before—I won't melt, you know."

"OK—OK, friend, have it your way," came the reply.

"My friends, something inside me tells me it is time to go to bed," mumbled a drowsy woodchuck as he rose and started for his doorway. "Goodnight to all. Br-r-r-r-r. My, that air is cold. Goodnight."

The little group broke up and each went about his own business. Porky decided that he was ready for bed too. Chatty headed for her hollow tree. Bertie sailed off to his favorite perch, and Doty Deer slipped silently away to her bed in the heavy brush.

Sly Fox decided to travel down toward the big river in search of a good supper. Bouncer Rabbit skipped happily away toward a distant pasture field where there grew a wonderful briar patch in which he and his cousins spent many happy and playful nighttime hours.

The chill air stirred by the wind from the east pepped up the energetic rabbit so that he grew more excited as he looked forward to a playful evening. All the while the hazy circle around the moon grew larger and larger.

Digby made his way down into his cozy bedroom and quickly curled up on his bed of dry leaves. The tiny voice from inside invited him to slumberland and soon he was fast asleep. His dreams were filled with memories of what had been, all-in-all, a good summer. He also dreamed of his many fine friends and the beautiful place in which they lived.

The night swirled past Digby's sleeping mind until suddenly he was aware that it must be morning. As he slowly awoke he sensed that something was different, but he could not decide what it was. After getting up from his bed and puttering around his living room for a few minutes, he realized in an instant that the silence was so deep and thick he could almost reach out and touch it. The cause of that terrible silence must be outside his house. He quickly headed for the front door.

Digby rushed up his hallway and plunged through the outside door. He had not stopped to check for danger as he usually did. In a moment he was slipping and sliding back down the hallway, wrapped in a great blanket of coldness.

"SNOW!" cried the startled groundhog at the top of his lungs as he fought to brush the fluffy whiteness from his eyes. "IT'S SNOWING IN MY HOUSE!"

Quickly he started pawing his way back up to the doorway. He made his way through mounds of snow and suddenly burst out into a blustery wind blowing harshly from the northeast—a wind filled with a heavy speckling of snowflakes. The world into which Digby had dashed was totally different from the one he had left the evening before.

The groundhog was not used to wading snow which reached a depth up to his back. Most years he was settled snugly in his house for the winter when snows like this one came. This year the entire meadow was taken by surprise.

Digby tried making his way down the hillside but the snow was so deep he decided just to go back to his house and settle in for the winter. At that moment, through the swirling snow, he could hear the voices of Ringo, Sly, Porky, and Bertie faintly calling, "Bouncer! Hey, Bouncer!"

"BOUNCER! Where are you-u-u-u?"

"Can you hear us, Bouncer?"

A chill of fear rippled down Digby's backbone. Now the deep snow made no difference. Down the hillside the fat groundhog went, stumbling, sliding, and struggling as fast as he could. At a very steep place in the trail he lost his footing and the last few yards of the trail he traveled much as a snowball would. The rolling, tumbling, snow-covered furry ball came to a stop at the very feet of those who had been calling for Bouncer.

"Wall, lookeee who comes rollin' in. Why I believe it's our good friend, ole snowball Digby," teased Porky Possum.

"OK, you smart-aleck possum, what's going on? Why are you calling for Bouncer?" panted the winded groundhog.

"We think he might be lost in the storm. At least he didn't come home last night," answered Ringo.

"We got worried and set out to look for him," chimed in Bertie.

"This snow is so deep we can't make very good time traveling," said Sly, who usually didn't have trouble moving around in the winter.

Digby's eyes lighted up, "Bertie, go find Doty. Her legs are long. She can break a trail for the rest of us."

"But where are we going to look for Bouncer?" inquired the crow.

"The briar patch in the pasture across the hill is the best place, I think," declared Sly, who in the old days chased rabbits there.

"But how in the world will we ever find him in this deep snow?" wondered Digby.

"I don't know, but we have to try," exclaimed Ringo.

Off flew Bertie to find Doty. In a few minutes the gentle-eyed deer came loping swiftly through the snow.

"Hurry, Doty, please lead us to the pasture. Bouncer may be lost. Please break a trail for the rest of us," voices in the crowd echoed.

"Follow me!" Doty called out as she started out toward the pasture.

Ringo spoke up, "Hey, where is Bertie? He didn't come back with you."

"He said he would be along shortly. He said he had some kind of bright idea."

The tiny band set off through the gloomy gray day with its spinning white curtain of snow. Doty broke the trail, but even at that it was very difficult going for the smaller ones. Not one stopped to rest though, that could wait until later.

As they reached the edge of the pasture, Bertie came swirling down out of the snow. "Hey! Look! I brought us some help."

"Hello, friends," came the voice of Mutt as he plunged through the snow toward them. "Can I help?"

"Bouncer is lost! You may be able to help with that hunting nose of yours," Digby explained.

"Maybe I can—just maybe I can. I hope so. Let's give it a try. Come on!" Mutt cried out.

"Where in the world do we begin to look?" asked the puzzled woodchuck.

"I suggest we begin over there by the briar patch. Start checking every clump of grass and weeds we come to. Always look on the side away from the wind. It was coming from the east, so look on the west side," Mutt advised. "If I know anything about Bouncer, he's not really lost. He just took the nearest shelter and crouched down when the storm came up so fast."

"Why didn't he come home before the storm? I will never understand," Bertie screeched.

"He must have had some good reason," commented Sly.

"Let's get started," called out Mutt as he began sniffing every clump of grass as he went. Everyone in the party started doing the same thing. It was slow going as they had to plow through the deep snow.

The hunt went on with only a frequent call to Bouncer from various ones of the searchers to be heard, along with the moaning of the cold wind to break the silence. Worry grew greater as the search went on without any success.

"Where are you, you foolish rabbit?" Digby worried out loud as he dug behind another tall clump of weeds. "Where are you? Oh! Where are you, Bouncer?"

"HEY! HEY! LOOK HERE!" cried out Mutt. "Look what I have found!"

In a moment the dog was surrounded by the others. There before their eyes could be seen the reason why Bouncer had not come in out of the storm. Peeking through the hole in the snow that Mutt had made was the calm, sleepy face of Bouncer Rabbit. And snuggled between his front paws could be seen a small gray field mouse curled up fast asleep and at peace with the world.

"Sh-h-h-h," cautioned Bouncer in a low voice, "he's had a bad night."

After a moment of amazement, the group began to laugh with relief, but not loud enough to disturb the sleeping mouse.

"RABBIT!" said Porky in a hushed voice but with some force, "Yo-all scared the tar out-a us, ya know, but I guess ya had a good reason."

Doty spoke up, "You know, it appears that Bouncer found a way to be a friend to someone in need even though it's in his nature to run away from danger."

"Just goes to show that anyone can do good things for others in their own way if they will only try. I learned that lesson through my own experience," Mutt said seriously.

Digby spoke up, "Bouncer, I think you should wake your little friend so we can start for home. It is mighty cold out here. The little fellow can ride on my back if he wishes, since the snow is far too deep for him. Bouncer, you know you are one great guy, but certainly you know how to make life a nervous experience at times."

Bouncer rolled his eyes and reminded Digby, "Hey, buddy, look who is talking. Who was it that was hit by a car because of his foolishness?"

Everybody had a good laugh. They loaded the little mouse on Digby's back where he could hold on by clutching the long fur there. And then the journey home began.

The trip back was a happy one. Not only because their friend had been found safe, but after waking him up, they found that Floyd Fieldmouse was a very nice fellow.

He accepted an invitation to stay the winter at Bouncer's house. His ability to carry on a fine conversation would provide the gabby rabbit with much company through the long winter.

After struggling through the drifts, the group came in sight of their snow-covered meadow home. As they did, Bouncer spoke up so all could hear.

"I have been thinking. You all came looking for me because you are my friends and you care about me. I protected Floyd during the storm because I wanted to be his friend. Now we are able to come home to our friendly meadow. Isn't it wonderful how things like that work? Digby talks now and then about that 'Whatever' that put us here and how It must be friendly because of all the good things we have from It. I believe that too. Whatever put us here is good, and I think when we are good to each other, It is happy." There was a round of comments from the group agreeing with Bouncer.

Digby wished everyone a happy, safe winter with warm homes to stay in. Then he made his way into his house and to his cozy bedroom. He made himself very comfortable for the long winter's nap ahead of him. With a smile on his face he closed his eyes and listened to the small, familiar voice from inside him, "Sleep, Digby—it's time to go to sleep now. You will find another wonderful summer and all your friends waiting for you when you wake up. Sleep now, Digby." And so he did.